TOMB RAIDER EMERITUS

TOMB RAIDER EMERITUS

I FEAR NO EVIL BOOK SIX

MARTHA CARR

MICHAEL ANDERLE

DISRUPTIVE IMAGINATION

TOMB RAIDER EMERITUS (this book) is a work of fiction.

All of the characters, organizations, and events portrayed in this novel are either products of the author's imagination or are used fictitiously. Sometimes both.

TOMB RAIDER EMERITUS TEAM

Thanks to the JIT Readers

John Ashmore
James Caplan
Peter Manis
Keith Verret
Mary Morris
Daniel Weigert
Larry Omans
Paul Westman

If we've missed anyone, please let us know!

From Martha

To everyone who still believes in magic
and all the possibilities that holds.
To all the readers who make this
entire ride so much fun.
And to my son, Louie and so many wonderful friends who
remind me all the time of what
really matters and how wonderful
life can be in any given moment.

From Michael

To Family, Friends and
Those Who Love
To Read.
May We All Enjoy Grace
To Live The Life We Are
Called.

Alison looked around the main room of Warehouse One for a few long moments before frowning and sticking her hands on her hips. "You need to put more powder on stuff. I can't see anything, Aunt Shay. I can see you, and those knives you have on you, but I can't see any of the obstacles."

Shay crossed her arms and shook her head. "No powder. All out. Too bad, so sad."

"Too bad, so sad? What are you, ten years old all of a sudden?" Alison laughed. "No, actually I think ten-year-olds have better insults."

With the recent victory of James in a court hearing to move ahead with his adoption of Alison and the defeat of the Drow queen Laena, the tension concerning the girl had lifted from everyone's shoulders. The ever-present threat of her being taken had vanished in a couple of short weeks. Now, the makeshift family could enjoy the rest of the summer without waiting for a Dark Elf ambush and spend time in such wholesome activities as tactical and obstacle training.

Shay rubbed her chin.

Maybe I can't train you until you're as good as me physically, kid, but you've got real magic, so you don't need to be as good. But we still need to make sure you're ready for all situations.

"Seriously, though, Alison. Not gonna use any powder."

Alison spun toward Shay and blinked. "No powder? How am I supposed to make out anything without the powder?"

The tomb raider grinned. "Yeah, now that you're officially and legally the daughter of *the* James Brownstone, I decided that I needed to make your training harder. In the real world, there's not always gonna be convenient magic powder on walls or obstacles to help you see things. The real world doesn't give a shit if you're blind." She shrugged. "That said, I'm still working on getting you an artifact to help you with your sight, but in the meantime, we need to focus more on your general situational awareness. Even when I get the artifact, you might end up losing it, and every weapon you have in your arsenal means a better chance of you coming out ahead in a difficult situation."

Alison shook her head. "At the rate you and Dad are going, you'll be shoving me out of an airplane and telling me to just sense when to pull the cord on my parachute."

"Don't give me any ideas."

"Have *you* jumped out of a plane?"

"A few times. It's a handy thing to get used to."

Alison laughed.

Shay wandered over to a tire-running obstacle. "I'm

wondering if you can cheat a little bit in the meantime. Before you get the artifact."

"Cheat?" Alison tilted her head slightly. "What do you mean?"

"Echolocation."

"Like a dolphin?" The teen's face scrunched in confusion.

"Yeah. It's something I've read about. Some blind humans do it, too. They can click their tongue and listen to the subtle sound differences. They use that to get a pretty good image in their heads of their environment. I saw a guy who could even differentiate different types of trees by the wood texture." Shay pointed at Alison. "The problem is you're just not blind enough."

"Not blind enough?" Alison laughed. "What do you mean? You were just talking about getting an artifact to help me see, and now you're saying I'm not blind enough? How blind do I need to be?"

Shay kicked one of the tires, enjoying the pushback against her boot. "I'm saying that because you've always had your soul sight and can see auras or soul energy or whatever you want to call it, you haven't had to develop the kind of skills that you would have if you were completely blind. Stuff like that echolocation. You're already able to fool most people as it is."

"Okay, I guess I can understand that." Alison shrugged. "So, what…you want me to start clicking my tongue or something? Become a human dolphin?"

The tomb raider shook her head. "No. I've got a better idea, but it was inspired by that idea. If you use a small amount of magic, it'll leave a light residue for a while, right?"

Alison nodded. "Depends on the magic, but yeah. What about it?"

"There's your echolocation or magolocation. Just send a small pulse of magic out, not all that directed. It doesn't have to be powerful or last long, just long enough that you can make out things for at least a second. Sure, it's gonna mean anyone else who can sense magic can track you, but if you're wandering around a mall or in the middle of a fight to the death, that's not gonna be a huge concern. This is just about giving you a new situational awareness tool."

The girl grinned. "Oh, I get it. I've spent so many years without realizing I could do magic that I never even thought about something like that." She shrugged. "No one suggested it at the school either, though I guess it wouldn't matter. It took me a while before I could see magic and not just soul and life energy."

Shay tapped her forehead. "Sometimes you just need a different perspective. I'm not a witch, so I don't think like one. The technique isn't a total substitute for being able to see your environment, but at least it would be a nice thing to develop. Another tool in your kit."

She wandered away from the obstacle to a table containing wooden swords. "You can see living things easily enough, which means you can fight somewhat, but a big part of fighting in the real world is using the environment, so we need to work on that. Try something now—a magolocation pulse. I'd give you advice, but it's not like I know shit about using magic other than artifacts."

Alison nodded and took a deep breath, then held her

hands to her sides palms-out and half-closed her eyes. A translucent lavender pulse blasted from her palms and passed through the room, fading as it moved.

Shay tensed but didn't feel anything as the light passed over her.

Sometimes I let myself forget that she's not just some teen, but she's a Drow princess. Someday she might even be more powerful than James.

"I think…" Alison sighed. "Okay, let me try again." She gritted her teeth and another pulse shot from her hands. "Okay. Not as easy as I'd hoped, but I can tell that you're standing by a table with some sticks on it."

"Wooden swords, but good job." Shay furrowed her brow. "Is there any way you can do that without making the light?"

Alison shrugged. "Maybe. I'll have to work on it."

"Guess it's not a big deal if you do it somewhere that's brightly lit. Most people probably won't even notice."

"If you say so."

"Can you still see the magic on the table?"

Alison frowned. "Yes, but it's fading really quickly. If I hadn't looked at the table before, I wouldn't be able to make out what it is, and if I use more magic so the residue lasts longer, it'll drain me pretty quick. Sending the big unfocused pulse is harder than I thought it'd be."

Shay smiled. "Doesn't matter. All in all, still a good start. Like I said, not a replacement for the artifact, but good in a pinch, and something to work on. I think it's more reliable than you trying to develop echolocation."

The girl raised her hands again and sent out another magical probe.

Shay picked up a sword and tossed it toward Alison, and the girl snatched it out of the air with ease. Not quite Lily, but damned impressive for someone who was blind.

"Good reflexes, kid." Shay picked up a wooden sword from the table. "We're not gonna go all-out in the fighting. Today I just wanted to see if you can use that trick to move around the room better. James' fancy tactical room has at least helped teach you the importance of cover in a fight, so we'll work on just being aware of where you are for now."

"Meaning what, exactly?"

The tomb raider held up the sword. "Can you see my sword?"

"No, but I can see your soul energy, and I can tell you're holding a sword from the way you're standing. It's something I've been practicing for a long time."

Shay grinned. "Good. Inference is a powerful tool in a fight too. I'm gonna chase you around a little, and I want you to evade. Try to find places where you can slow me down but keep your weapon in hand at all times. If you lose your weapon in a fight, you're done."

Alison frowned. "Not sure if I can get a good image using just one hand."

"That's a good limitation to know and practice then. Sometimes when I'm doing raids, there are environmental limitations. If I'm gonna go underwater, for example, I know I can't rely on my standard weapons. I have to predict, adapt, and overcome the challenges if I don't want to get hurt."

"I'm not going to be a tomb raider." The girl chuckled. "At least I don't think I'm going to be. Although I'm not going to be a bounty hunter either, Dad keeps having me do bounty-hunter training."

Shay stalked toward Alison, smirking and raising her weapon. "It doesn't matter. I didn't think I was gonna be a tomb raider when I was your age either. We never know what the future's gonna bring."

Alison backed away. She lifted a free hand and emitted another pulse before pointing her hand behind her and doing it again. She turned and rushed toward a raised sparring ring Shay had set up in a corner.

Good girl. I didn't even tell you to try to go there.

The tomb raider grinned and jogged after her. The teen rolled through the bottom ropes with ease and hopped to her feet.

She shot Shay a grin. "I don't know how long I can keep this up, but it's fun. If I were being chased, I could blast my attackers with magic, too."

"True, but today isn't about blasting away with magic." The tomb raider hopped into the ring and over the ropes and swung at Alison. The clack of the girl's wooden sword meeting Shay's echoed in the warehouse.

Shay took another swing. Alison dodged it this time.

"Can you see the sword, or are you reading my body again?" the tomb raider asked.

"Reading the body." Alison thrust forward, and Shay blocked the attack.

"It's great having you home for summer break. James isn't as mopey as he usually is. It makes everything more fun."

Alison laughed and tried two quick swings, but Shay blocked them with ease. She could knock the sword out of the girl's hand if she wanted to, but she wanted the teen to get used to the idea of situational awareness and the new technique before they started drilling more hardcore. Humiliating her wouldn't help in this situation.

"Dad isn't mopey, he's just a thoughtful introvert."

Shay burst out laughing. "That has to be the first time that someone has ever described James Brownstone as a thoughtful introvert."

Alison took several quick steps back and held her hand to the side to send another pulse. She hopped over the ropes and out of the ring, and once she hit the ground, she ran toward a climbing rope that led to a raised platform.

"He just has trouble expressing his feelings, is all," she called over her shoulder. "I think he doesn't realize what a good man he is. I keep telling him, but he thinks I'm just making stuff up."

Yeah, James loves himself some Catholic guilt, that's for sure.

The tomb raider rolled under the ropes and returned to her feet. "That we can agree on, kid."

Alison leaped onto the rope and grabbed it with her free hand while she gripped the sword in the other. She scooted up the rope at a decent clip with the help of her feet. It was an awkward movement with a wooden sword in hand, but if she'd been holding a gun, she would have been able to return fire without too much trouble.

Good tactical instincts. You can't teach that.

The platform led to a series of swinging ropes, so Shay waited for Alison to reach the platform, then jumped onto the rope herself to follow the girl.

The teen wobbled at the edge, and Shay hissed. She

didn't have most of the safety mats out. She hadn't planned on the girl taking on the higher obstacles that day.

The tomb raider climbed faster. "Can you see the obstacles still?"

"No, but I've got a pretty good idea where they are." Step after step, Alison moved closer to the edge.

Should I say something? She's supposed to have situational awareness, but shit, if she falls she could break something. I've got a healing potion, but that's a pretty expensive lesson, and James will be pissed.

Damn it.

Shay crested the platform, her heart pounding as Alison danced near the edge. One of the girl's feet moved over the edge, her foot lowering itself toward nothing but air.

"Careful," the tomb raider shouted. "You're about to fall."

Alison stood there on one foot, a grin on her face. She waved her sword and waggled her other foot. "You know what the guys at Camp Brownstone would say about this situation?"

Shay took a deep breath and shook her head. "What?"

"All warfare is based on deception." Alison hopped back to the center of the platform and sent out another pulse. "Just wanted to mess with you a little, Aunt Shay."

The tomb raider rolled her eyes. "Cute, kid. Very cute. Annoying, too. Just so you know."

Alison rested the sword on her shoulder. "I appreciate what you and Dad are trying to do with all this training, and a lot of it's been helpful or just fun." She shrugged. "But I do think that sometimes you guys forget I'm not a little girl who needs to be protected from all risks."

Yeah, you just whined to your dad about having to do phys-ical training at the start of your vacation. Then again...

Shay chuckled. At Alison's age, she was already murdering people for money. The girl did have a point. Her handicap was a disadvantage in some situations, but an advantage in others.

The tomb raider shrugged. "We know you're not a little girl, but we just want to do what we can to make sure you're able to take care of yourself. You're getting older, and you're not always gonna be somewhere we can protect you. We both know how dangerous this world is, especially because of your heritage."

"I know, and it's good to have family who cares."

The word "family" lingered in Shay's mind for a few seconds.

Family? Is that what this is? Is that why I'm bothering to show this girl I have no relation to all this when I didn't care about my blood family? Why I worry about her at school? Why I killed men to protect her?

James taught me I could love, but with Alison, it's a different sort of thing. Caring about someone else and wanting to improve them, rather than them being a partner or lover.

Shay blew out a breath. She hated epiphanies. They were so annoying.

Alison blinked. "Something wrong, Aunt Shay?"

"Not really...just thinking. We already covered how you're not gonna be a tomb raider. Maybe. Have you thought much about your plans for after school?"

"Not sure, to be honest. I hadn't spent a lot of time thinking about what I might do when I was an adult. I always thought being blind meant I couldn't have a normal job."

Shay scoffed. "Screw normal jobs. You're a half-Drow princess who can see souls. Get a cool job, not a normal job."

Alison laughed. "Like what, bounty hunting or tomb raiding?"

"I don't know. I'm sure you'll figure something out, kid."

"And if I asked you to start training me as a tomb raider?"

Shay snickered. "I'm sure your dad would have a few choice words for me, and a boot he'd stick up my ass."

"Then what about something just a little less dangerous? What about parkour?"

"I don't know, Alison." The tomb raider rubbed the back of her neck. "That's a lot of movement and a long way to fall."

Alison shrugged. "But I can do the pulse."

"Maybe we can talk about it in the future when we've got the vision artifact." Shay laughed. "Then I can be the woman who taught the blind girl parkour."

"Is that better or worse than training a teen to be a tomb raider?"

Shay shrugged, but her smile slowly faded.

So teaching Alison is silly, but training Lily isn't? Shit, I've brought her on tomb raids with me already. She can see, but maybe Alison would have been able to see those invisible ghosts in England with her powers.

Damn it. I'm worried about Alison and making sure she's safe, but I'm letting Lily live underground by her own choice. Wonder what she's up these days? It's been a while.

She sighed.

What a complicated damned world.

A few hours later, Shay climbed a rolling ladder toward one of her stacks in Warehouse Four. She had a little additional background research she needed to do for a lecture at the university tomorrow. Her hand glided along until she found the title in question, and she pulled it from the stack and moved down the ladder.

She turned to leave but stopped and glanced back over her shoulder with a frown, her thoughts from earlier in the day about Lily bubbling up again.

Alison lost her parents but ended up with a rich if rough guardian and a beautiful and badass aunt. Lily only has those other kids.

Maybe it's not my business to give a shit about the girl, but I do, and the least I can do is help a little with her education.

Shay walked over to a different section of the library. Time to grab a few books for Lily. Maybe she could stop by the tunnels and chat with her.

2

Shay smiled at the gathered students in the UCLA lecture hall. It was time to drop some more truth and open some minds. Maybe giving lectures wasn't as exciting as slicing up a bunyip or taking on ghosts, but it was far less likely to end with her head bitten off or soul siphoned away. Always needed to look at the advantages and disadvantages.

A lot of students here today, and even a professor or two. Not bad. My academic rep must be growing on campus. Badass killer. Badass tomb raider. Badass professor.

A wide grin replaced her smile. Triple threat.

The gathered students were all older than Lily and Alison. More than a few were older than Shay, but she found she had no less desire to pass on her hard-earned wisdom to them.

The university was a place that was about your achievements, not your age. In a sense, it was similar to tomb raiding.

"Religion, myth, history, legend," Shay intoned. "We like

to tell ourselves these things are different, how the categories vary in truth and meaning. That's how scholars were taught to think for decades, but we know now that viewpoint was myopic to the say the least—and downright stupid in many cases."

Several students nodded their agreement. A few others frowned or laughed. Being provocative was always a good way to start a lecture. She'd started doing it more and more. What was the worst thing that could happen? Someone was offended? Big deal.

Shay cut through the air with her hand. "But if Oriceran has taught us anything, it's that we have no business blithely declaring what's true and what's a mere story, not anymore. We need to make sure we don't ever again fall into the arrogant pattern of thinking we know with absolute certainty what the truth is and that we've uncovered all the relevant evidence. We can get close, but there might be some other piece of information out there we don't know about. That should always be at the back of our minds, taunting us. In a world where magic is real, the possibilities are endless."

The eager students in the front row leaned forward, their eyes locked on her. Even though the lectures weren't for credit, it seemed like more students attended each new session. Shay couldn't help but be pleased with that. It was always pleasant to be reminded she was good at something other than kicking ass and snatching old artifacts out of moldy dungeons.

Maybe if I'd known about this when I was a teen, I wouldn't have spent ten years killing people and thinking that was the only thing I was good at.

"We know now that a number of the ancient myths we associate with the religions and folk beliefs of cultures worldwide are based on rock-solid historical truth, like most of what we called history until a few decades ago." Shay pressed a button on the remote in her hand. The PowerPoint slide with her lecture title *An Indian Atlantis: A Revised History Examination of Old Dwarka* was replaced by a map of southern Asia and the Middle East. An island was marked just off the western coast of India.

Shay nodded toward the screen. "India is one of the oldest centers of civilization on Earth. Setting aside our previous archaeologist examinations of the ruins of ancient cultures there, we also have various Hindu scriptures and epics providing evidence.

"Before Oriceran, most non-Hindu scholars interpreted these sources as mere metaphors or reinterpretations of non-supernatural events, but we now know that at least some of these events did occur, and were magical in nature. Although there remains significant controversy about the exact meaning and truth of specific incidents in ancient legend and religion, we can't, no matter our personal beliefs, so easily set aside traditional explanations of events without risking missing out on the fundamental truth of ancient events."

She advanced a slide, revealing an elaborate image of the blue-skinned Lord Krishna sitting on a throne with a flute, a satisfied smile on his face.

A few images here and there were the spice of a lecture, but like a meal, too much spice could make things hard to swallow. She preferred to rely on her words.

Shay nodded toward the slide. "An ancient myth speaks

of a mighty city, Dwarka, off India's Saurashtra coast. A modern city bears that name, but this was an older city, that I'll refer to as Old Dwarka. The city was on an island that was alleged to have earned the wrath of Lord Krishna around four thousand years ago. As a result of his displeasure, he let the entire island sink into the Arabian Sea as a lesson to all who would make a mockery of their *dharma*, which I'll horribly simplify here and reduce to the right way of living according to the cosmic order. So, this was, in a sense, a city being punished for being sinful if you want to think of it that way."

The ever-eager Mary, who was sitting in the front row, shot her hand up.

"Yes, Mary?"

The girl furrowed her brow. "And there's no overlap between this and the legend of Atlantis? It's not just the other legend being reworked to fit in with local culture? The parallels are amazing."

Shay shook her head. "Some scholars in the past argued that it was the result of some sort of cultural diffusion via Macedonian transmission of existing Greek legends of Atlantis, but the details are different, and now we know for certain that these refer to discrete events which just happened to be similar. The timing of the appearance of the legends and the events they reference is different.

"If you think about it, there's a lot of water on the Earth, and the oceans are pretty deep. Even if you ignore cities being teleported wholesale using magic and that kind of thing, there's just a lot of land that the oceans have swallowed, and we're now just finding out about it. Atlantis and

Dwarka aren't the only cities lost to the hungry maw of the sea."

Shay advanced a slide. A radar satellite image highlighted a submerged island just off the coast of India.

"Thanks to modern technology, we now know there's definitely a lost city in the sea near the present-day Dwarka. Originally, archaeologists thought the cities were part of the same settlement, but more recent data indicate that the sea ruins have numerous architectural and other material differences that reveal they are somewhat independent sites. There was a clear and cataclysmic break in the material and social nature of local civilization, which is consistent with the sudden sinking of an island containing a city-state as detailed in the legend.

"Ancient cities had a lot more than just buildings, people, and livestock, especially powerful and advanced ancient cities, though, so I'm going to talk about what I think you are *really* interested in." Shay advanced a slide to a picture of piles of jewels, idols, and gold.

The students murmured and let out a few appreciative laughs. One frat boy in the back clapped.

"Now for the fun part." Shay grinned. "As I hinted, the island and city didn't just go down with a few boring buildings and some sheep. The legends state they went down with a pile of Lord Krishna's treasure. This was alleged to have been purposeful to reflect his concern over the shortsightedness of the inhabitants." She shrugged. "That said, very little of said treasure has been recovered in the decades since the discovery of the older city."

A student raised his hand in the back. Shay pointed at him.

"How do we even know there is any treasure?" the student asked. "I mean, anyone can claim there's treasure somewhere, but that doesn't mean there is."

"Good question, and good point. They have found just enough to make them think there is more, especially in terms of precious metals and jewels. Given the nature of magic and people's different understandings concerning magical artifacts at different points in history, we can't be certain that magical items weren't looted from the site previously. Some magical surveys have suggested residual pockets of magic energy that might be associated with artifacts, which naturally leads us to ask about what else can we glean from ancient sources about this mysterious lost city?"

Shay walked over to her lectern and picked up a vacuum-sealed bag containing an old and yellowed tome with an elaborately decorated cover depicting several Hindu gods and demons in battle, with a few vimanas in the sky raining down lightning. Gold and silver-inscribed Sanskrit writing decorated the front.

I can't believe I got this for only fifty pounds. Almost feel bad for the poor sucker who sold it to me. Talk about a steal.

She held up the book. "This is four hundred years old. Our country isn't even that old."

A collective gasp swept the audience.

"But even after thinking about how old it is, it's important to realize this is just a hand-copied version of a far more ancient text. This book was discovered in a tiny little bookstore in London. The owners thought it was a copy of the *Rigveda* and never bothered to get it translated, which was unfortunate for them. It was recovered by a…freelance collector who had it translated. She discovered that it provides previously unrevealed details of the events leading to the sinking of old Dwarka."

Yeah, don't want to let these students know I have a massive hidden library of ancient books. That might raise a few too many questions about how a newly minted professor could afford something like that.

"The book suggests that the sinking of Old Dwarka was less a direct punishment of Lord Krishna, but rather the result of the people and non-divine beings involved ignoring his warnings about following dharma. Thus, their actions led to the same outcome.

"Interestingly, the tale related in this book is one that I think any modern person, magical or otherwise, would find familiar. There were multiple factions in the ancient society, with increasing tensions between two of the main ones in the decades preceding the sinking. That is to say, there was no sudden cataclysm, but more a slow-motion disaster that people could have seen and avoided."

Shay set the book down, rested an elbow on the lectern, and nodded up at a new slide revealing a rather stylized battle involving everything from chariots to a saucer-shaped vimanas performing a strafing run with blue and orange lightning bolts.

"The book doesn't detail the exact nature of the tensions, only that they concerned the disposition of a rare resource. Some scholars suggested it might be something like adamantine. Others have suggested unusually powerful magical artifacts and who should be using them. In any event, even if we don't know what they were fighting about, we do know that in the end, they formed two opposing armies and waged a final massive battle using powerful magic, probably some of the strongest in the world at that time."

The next PowerPoint slide was simple and straightforward: a mushroom cloud. Maybe it wasn't all that accurate depiction of the aftermath of the battle, but it got the point across.

Silence choked the lecture hall. The audience was hanging on her every word.

Yeah, I'm good.

"Powerful elemental magic was used by both sides, but according to the book, which recounts the stories of a few survivor-refugees, the spells on both sides were more effective than expected because of synergistic interactions. Massive earthquakes and volcanic eruptions helped sink the island, and also raised the level of the sea to swallow what was left. So, the story ends like so many on this planet end, with short-sighted greed destroying everyone involved. No winners. No losers. Only a handful of survivors."

Shay nodded to the book. "We're just beginning to untangle the truth of those long-ago events, but there's still a lot to learn." She took a deep breath. "Now, do you have any questions?"

Mary raised her hand. "You just talked about elemental magic, but now that we have wizards, witches, and Oricerans, can't they help reveal the exact nature of the magic? Not that I want them to use the same spells, but if they could tell us more about the magic used, then we'd get closer to the truth of how the city and island were destroyed."

Shay shook her head. "Most magical people aren't all that interested in the site, and even then, it's not that easy for a wizard to figure out the kind of magic used in a battle thousands of years ago. Initial investigations have confirmed that powerful magic was used on the old city and the island, but that's all we know."

A huge male student Shay didn't recognize raised his hand in the back.

"Yes?"

"So, like, you mentioned the treasure earlier. Are you saying that there could be piles of gold or super-powerful magical artifacts there, and no one has found them yet?"

Shay nodded. "That's exactly what I'm saying. The thing is, even with magic to help, archaeology, let alone underwater archaeology, can be hard. Damned difficult, even. There hasn't been much interest in exploring the site, even though some are worried about curses or other dark magic that might have been left over from the destruction of the island."

He frowned. "But curses are BS, right?"

The tomb raider shook her head. "Some are, but a lot aren't. Many archaeologists in the late nineteenth and early twentieth centuries got lucky that the low level of magic on Earth limited the power of the curses associated with some of the sites they investigated. For example, if Tut's tomb had been found in the modern magical environment, every last person associated with that dig would most likely have been dead within days."

Most of the class gasped at that.

Mary shook her head. "It's just strange to think about how much more there is still to learn about this world."

Shay nodded. "That's exactly what I want you all to take away from these lectures. Remember, you should be happy that we found out about Oriceran. Happy that there's a whole new frontier of knowledge to challenge your mind. Also remember that although many myths and legends have turned out to be true, there's no guarantee that they all are."

Several more hands shot up, and Shay grinned.

Damn. I love this.

Shay chuckled as she walked toward the parking lot. The modest sedan she had driven to the university was a far cry from her Fiat. She was half-tempted to just start driving the sports car and feed everyone the same line she'd once given her friends—that a rich boyfriend had given it to her —but she decided driving another car to the university would be a better bet.

If there was one lesson Shay had internalized in her life, including her decade as a brutal killer, it was that the more ornate a lie, the easier it was to see through it. People craved the easy to understand, the banal. Anything that stepped outside those boundaries upset their carefully balanced world and made them start wanting to look deeper.

There was no reason for her to give them a reason to do that.

Shay blew out a breath and checked the area as she rounded a corner. There wasn't a single person around. Even though she was now living more openly, she couldn't let her guard down when she was about to drive to a warehouse. The only people who knew the locations were those she could trust with her life, and although she'd destroyed the Nuevo Gulf Cartel, she had a long list of other enemies who might love a chance to kill her or destroy her warehouses.

Don't know if I'll ever be able to let my guard down entirely. James is an utter badass who wasted a bunch of Harriken, and he still had assholes who blew up his house with a rocket launcher before people bought a clue. And he was trying to spread his reputation around, unlike me.

She pulled out her phone and dialed Peyton.

"What's up?" he answered cheerfully.

"I just gave a lecture at the university."

"That go well?"

Shay grinned. "My lectures always go well. When I set out to do something, I don't do it half-assed. I'm sure most of these kids will change their majors to revised history or archaeology if they haven't already. A lot of them aren't even from the department, or at least I don't think they are."

Peyton chuckled. "Humble much?"

"I don't believe in false humility. Anyway, I was just giving a lecture on the city of Old Dwarka. I did some background research on it for the lecture, and everything I've found suggests there's treasure to be found there. I'm beginning to think I should check it out."

"Old Dwarka. Isn't that the place that's underwater?"

Shay scoffed. "I've got a lot of dive gear."

Peyton laughed. "Yeah, and you bitch a lot about having to do stuff underwater."

"Touché. Just start looking into it. I've got a decent pile of cash from all my tomb raids, even with the recent warehouse upgrades. Aletheia has an established reputation now, meaning I can pursue a personal opportunity here or there."

A crunch came over the line.

Shay frowned. "What the hell was that? Did you just break something?"

"Potato chips."

"You couldn't have waited to eat?"

Peyton chuckled. "You called in the middle of my snack. You're the one with bad timing, not me."

Shay rolled her eyes. "Whatever. Just start doing background research on Old Dwarka. Not sure it'll be our next raid, but there'll be no patron this time, and we'll keep what I find. I really need to get my own arsenal of artifacts, so I'll have more options."

"Not disagreeing. Sounds like a good plan."

"I'll let you go back to your chips now, Peyton. Enjoy, and don't choke on them."

He laughed. "Thanks."

Shay ended the call.

If I want to have any chance of dealing with people like Yulia, I need to bring a lot more artifacts with me. It's time for the next step in my career or for me to walk away, and I don't feel like walking away.

Shay tensed as movement caught her attention. Someone was sprinting toward her.

3

The tomb raider narrowed her eyes and widened her stance. Even though she was in a skirt and button-up blouse for her lecture rather than something more practical—let alone tactical—she had a knife concealed in her skirt and a gun in her purse. That was one thing she could always say about when she needed to carry a bag of some sort. They were great places to hide weapons.

Shay gritted her teeth.

Don't ruin my day, asshole. I was having a nice post-lecture buzz, and I don't want to have to explain away a body on campus. It took me too much effort to get established here.

Shay rolled her eyes and snickered as the form closed on her. The battle would need to be postponed. It wasn't an assassin, or at least she didn't know of an assassin who'd be caught dead in khaki pants, a cardigan, and a bowtie.

She sighed and let her shoulders relax, even if her stomach was still knotted. In a sense, the man might be more dangerous than an assassin. It was her department head.

What the hell does he *want? He wasn't even at my lecture.*

"Professor Carson," the man called. He arrived at her car and bent over, puffing and red-faced. He needed to get in more regular cardio if a little jog like that had him suffering so much.

Shay gave him a polite nod. "Hello, Doctor Weber. In a rush, I see."

Dr. Weber took a few more seconds to catch his breath before straightening. "Yes. I just had something to ask you about. Something that I wanted to do in a semi-private setting, which is why I didn't just come to the end of your lecture to ask you about it."

Shay shrugged. "Okay. I was on my way home, but ask away."

"It's just…" He sighed and looked away. "I've sat in on a few of your lectures and, of course, I reviewed your previous material. Your understanding of revised history to archaeology, especially for someone so early in your career…well, it's unparalleled. When you lecture, it's often like you've been to these places. I can really feel your passion for your work."

Been to more of them than you realize. Maybe not doing careful archaeology, but I definitely was grabbing a piece or two of the past.

Shay took a deep breath. The problem with a career, even a fake career, was that it exposed her to office politics. She couldn't handle the department head the way she might handle an annoying triad member on the street or even just a typical person who bothered her.

She had to give him respect, even if she didn't necessarily believe he deserved it.

"I'm glad you understand my passion for my work. Is there anything else, sir?" Shay looked at him expectantly.

Dr. Weber cleared his throat. Even though he was no longer huffing and puffing, his face was still bright red as if he were embarrassed.

"It's just that I think you display insight into certain archaeological sites that more mainstream scholars might not know a lot about. Even after these past two decades, it's hard for a lot of people in our field and related fields to accept the paradigm change that Oriceran demands." He shook his head. "A good scholar should, of course, but a man who spent decades arguing one position isn't likely to want to say he was wrong. Not that I can blame them."

Shay crossed her arms and frowned. The good doctor was taking an awfully long time to get to anything approaching a point, and she really wanted to get to Warehouse Two.

She sighed. "Again, not something I disagree with, Doctor, but I don't see what this has to do with me."

He looked over his shoulder as if afraid he might be overheard. "You're right. I should get to the point."

"It would be helpful, yes."

"Do you know anything about the Anzick burial site in Montana?"

Shay nodded. "That's not that obscure a place. It's part of the original Clovis Complex."

"Is that all you know about it? You seem to specialize in European and Asian history, so I wasn't sure about your knowledge of Pre-Colombian North American history."

She offered him a shrug. "It's a Native American burial site generally dated to around thirteen thousand years ago.

Who the hell knows, given some of the issues with magic affecting carbon dating. Most traditional archaeologists suggest the Clovis people were the link between Asian populations and modern Native Americans, and much of the genetic evidence backs that up. There's also evidence to suggest that they or their ancestors might have traveled via a land bridge between Asia and North America, though there are still a lot of competing theories out there."

Dr. Weber bit his lip and gave her a shallow nod. "That's generally accurate. The thing is…"

Fuck. Can this guy be any less efficient? I'm sure his students must hate his lectures if this is how he delivers them.

"The thing is what, Dr. Weber?"

Again, he checked over his shoulder as if expecting a hitman to pop from behind a car and take him out.

"There are certain inconsistencies with some of the artifacts, beyond dating issues. I've been studying that culture and the site for thirty years, and prior to this I just wondered if we were missing something." He looked down at his shoes. "But…"

Shay sighed. Part of her wanted to tell him to go away so she could head back to Warehouse Two and talk to Peyton about a Dwarka tomb raid, but another part of her wanted to hear more about whatever mystery Dr. Weber thought he'd uncovered.

After all, a good part of a reason she lectured at the school was that she enjoyed history. In the end, simple curiosity, along with a desire not to annoy her department head, kept her in place.

She gestured for Dr. Weber to continue.

The man looked up and nodded. "Well, you see, a lot of

those inconsistencies concerning the land bridge or other theories might be resolved if we took into account something else. Something that should be included as part of the modern archaeology and revised history paradigm."

"Can you be more specific?"

"Well, not to put too fine a point on it, but something that might facilitate quick travel between distant locations…"

Shay lifted her eyebrows. "You think it was a magical portal?"

Excitement filled Dr. Weber's face. "Exactly. It's something I haven't dared talk about for a long time. When my career was starting, I almost destroyed it by talking about how it might be something of that nature. It was only because I had a few mentors of influence that I wasn't laughed out of the field completely. My wife begged me to stop talking about it, so I did." He blew out a breath. "But now, with Oriceran, that changes everything. I think the site holds information about early human contact with Oricerans, but I need someone to lead the dig who has expertise in revised history. Otherwise, they might miss vital clues."

The tomb raider blinked. "Wait, you want me to go check out the site?"

"Yes, and some related sites where we know there might be artifacts that have yet to be excavated."

Shay shrugged. "That sounds expensive, and as you know, I'm not exactly swimming in grant money. After all, I only deliver guest lectures here."

Dr. Weber nodded. "Oh, of course, but I have funds I could direct your way. I *am* the department head, after all.

If you're interested in following up on this, I could make sure the dig was fully funded, and…" he leaned forward and lowered his voice, "this might be a good intro toward getting a permanent faculty position."

She resisted a snort.

The amount of money I make on one tomb raid could fund the average archaeology dig for years, and I'm not ready to quit the day job and teach fulltime.

She sighed. "The thing is, Dr. Weber, I'm not in a position right now to commit to any long-term excavation projects. Between my lectures at the school and various personal projects, I can't agree to it, no matter how interesting I find the idea."

Disappointment spread over his face. "Oh, of course. I understand, but will you at least keep it in mind?"

Shay smiled. "That I can do."

"Excellent." Dr. Weber shrugged. "I've waited thirty years. It's not like waiting a year or two more will hurt me. Thank you for your time, Professor Carson."

The department head slunk off down the sidewalk and away from the parking lot.

Shay blew out a breath and shook her head. As much as she loved uncovering truths, she wasn't a real professor, and a few fun lectures now and again wasn't the same thing as having time to do a professional—which by its nature was slow and methodical—archaeological dig.

She headed toward her car.

Interesting story, though. Maybe something to check out in the future.

Shay stepped out of the car in the bay at Warehouse Two and headed toward the office, a purse over one shoulder and a satchel containing her book over the other. She blinked and smiled at a familiar teen perched on the edge of Peyton's desk. It'd been far too long since she'd talked to Lily.

The teen grinned at Peyton, who was sitting in his chair. "Come on, you never know. You might like it. Just think about trying it. Don't be such an old man. Shay does it, and she's older than you."

The hacker shook his head. "I'm not crazy like you and Shay. I don't need to jump off buildings. I like living, and I cherish every single second of my life. No pointless risks for me."

"Boring." Lily stretched out the word.

A delicious scent hung in the air, along with the extra heat that came from using the pizza oven.

I thought he'd never be able to do anything, but he's approaching becoming the Pizza King in truth. I've rarely been happier to be wrong about something.

Shay walked over to the office. "What's up, you two? What are you trying to peer-pressure Peyton into?"

Lily shrugged. "Trying to get Peyton interested in parkour, but he's going full grandpa on me."

He rolled his eyes. "I have enough danger in my life. I don't need to add more."

Shay chuckled and turned to Lily. "It's been a while since I last saw you. You don't look panicked or like you have to hide from gangsters."

The girl shrugged. "I'm fine. Everything's going well.

The money you've paid me has made it easy to keep everyone in food without scavenging."

"You earned that money—every penny. Not that I'm upset that you're here, but why are you here?"

"Just stopped by to see if there were any jobs and if you wanted to work out later. Even with the parkour, it's just not the same without you."

Shay furrowed her brow. There was nothing wrong with taking Lily to Warehouse One for a little workout, but something tugged at the back of her mind. A small twinge of guilt, especially with Alison in town. Spending time training a secret protégé she'd hidden from James and Alison felt a little bit weird, and even a little wrong.

Fuck. I probably should tell them about her sooner rather than later, but I just have to figure out the best way to do that. It's not like she's a secret kid from a previous marriage or something. They don't have a cartel or gangsters after them. At least not anymore.

The tomb raider shrugged. "I'm sure something can be arranged. Not sure about jobs. Things have been a bit dry lately on that front. I've got Peyton looking into a potential job, but we need to do a little background research on the site." She sniffed the air. "Setting that aside, something smells damned wonderful, Peyton."

Peyton grinned and stood. The sight wiped the smile off Shay's face. The man's pants were an abomination—shiny gold stripes and whorls over red spandex and flared bottoms. It wasn't just unfashionable, it was anti-fashion. A sartorial sin.

Shay groaned. "So which of you is Starsky?"

Peyton and Lily exchanged looks.

"Huh?" was Peyton's brilliant reply. "Starsky?"

Lily just shrugged.

Shay waved a hand. "No respect for the classics."

Captain Anti-Fashion marched over to the pizza oven, grabbed his paddle, and pulled out a mouth-watering thin-crust pepperoni pizza. Being good at cooking pizza went a long way toward making up for his unfortunate clothing choices.

Shay licked her lips and then blinked as Peyton deposited the pizza on a tray next to eight other pizzas on a nearby table. Each had a single slice removed.

Shay gestured to the table. "Are we having a rave or something you didn't tell me about? Or is James stopping by and worried about making weight for a new pro-wrestling career he hasn't told me about?"

Lily snickered.

Peyton shook his head. "Nope. I wanted to perfect the flour-to-water ratio, so I needed to do a few experiments. Well, more than a few, because things just weren't right." He pointed to one of the older pizzas. "None of my test slices were quite right, but I figure Lily can take the pizzas back to her underground lair to share with her special underdweller friends."

Lily rolled her eyes. She reached into her pocket and pulled out a paperclip. With the precision of a Marine Corps Force Recon sniper, she pelted the hacker in the head.

"Ow." Peyton rubbed his head. "That hurt."

Shay laughed. "Don't pick a fight you can't win, Peyton."

Osiris took advantage of the distracted humans to snatch a pizza from the table and drag it away. The cat stopped and tilted his head. A mouse grabbed a free piece of pepperoni and scurried off with it. The cat dropped the pizza and sprinted after the rodent with a yowl. Instinct fueled his active hunt.

Shay winced. Nothing should be getting into the warehouse, including mice, but it wasn't like she could call a normal pest control company. After a moment, she shrugged. The cat would finally earn its keep. Not a bad deal.

Lily snorted at Peyton. "'Underdwellers?' Seriously?"

Peyton shrugged. "Is that not politically correct? What should I be calling them, 'tunnel rats?'"

"Don't make me hurt you," Lily warned. "I wonder what your little girlfriend would think if she knew what you actually did for a living. Of course, knowing you, someday you'll want to give her a tour of your office at the warehouse to try to impress her, and you'll tell her how you're the ultimate hacker and all that."

"Hey, now, that's not funny."

Shay removed her gun from her purse and slapped it on the table. Peyton and Lily snapped their heads in her direction.

Frowning, the tomb raider rested her hand lightly on the gun and smiled. "Just remember, no one gets access to or told the location of any of the warehouses without my explicit permission." She narrowed her eyes at Peyton. "I don't care how nerd-sexy they are." Her gaze slid to Lily. "Or if you trust them with your life. Even good and trustworthy people can give up information they don't want to, depending on the situation."

Peyton swallowed. "Always nice to be reminded who's

the cat and who are the mice." He tilted his head at the satchel she had over her other shoulder. "What's that?"

Shay frowned. She didn't like her threats dismissed so easily. She looked down at the satchel and noticed the vacuum bag containing the book on the Dwarka was poking out of the top.

"It's a book on Old Dwarka. It's in Sanskrit, but I have an app with the translation, so I can read it line by line and sync it with the illustrations. You'd be surprised what kind of useful information you can find in illustrations."

Peyton shrugged. "They do say a picture is worth a thousand words." He chuckled. "And yet again, you've brought me major background info before I could really get going."

Lily peered at the bag. "This is the job you were talking about earlier? Where is it?"

Shay opened her mouth, but a fog horn blasted from Peyton's computer. He rushed back into the office and sat down to check the computer.

"Please tell me you've got good news," Shay called to him. "I don't really want my day ruined by having to go threaten or kill someone. It's been a good day."

Peyton grinned and shook his head. "Nope. Not that kind of alarm. Job alarm. Somebody needs a tomb raider of your quality, or at least your pay range."

Shay snickered. "Okay, now I like what I'm hearing. It's about time. Been fun to play around with Alison, but I need to bring home some treasure before I get rusty."

"One second." Peyton frowned and quickly skimmed the information in the alert.

Shay crossed her arms and tapped her foot. Lily

bounced back and forth on one foot, excitement on her face.

Guess I'm not the only one who wanted a little tomb-raiding excitement. Guess ultra-parkour still isn't as interesting as tomb raiding.

Peyton blew out a breath and nodded "Okay. The TL/DR is that they want you to recover the Necessaire Egg."

Lily frowned. "Is this egg guarded by a demonic chicken?"

Shay snorted. "Good question. Is it?"

Peyton shook his head. "No demonic chickens, at least in the initial alert. I haven't had time to confirm all the details. Anyway, it's one of the seven lost Imperial Faberge eggs of the original fifty-two made for the tsars. It's a jeweled egg decorated in diamonds. It was made to hold women's toiletries, which were also decorated in diamonds, by the way."

"Masters and mistresses of bling. Got it. Those tsarinas knew how to rock a bathroom. How much is the job paying?"

A grin split Peyton's face. "They're offering twenty million for its recovery."

Damn. That would more than pay for all my recent warehouse upgrades and then some. Still, something smells off here.

Lily whistled.

The tomb raider frowned. "That's a big payday, even for one of those. Sure, it's worth a lot, but most haven't sold for anywhere near that much. There's something else going on here. Hiring a tomb raider for that much to grab lost jewelry is overkill." She pointed at Peyton. "A little test of your skills. Find out what you can in the next hour, and we'll reconvene to figure out if demonic chickens are involved and what else is going on."

Peyton nodded. "And what are you going to do while I'm doing research?"

Shay smiled. "Eat some pizza before your damned cat steals it all."

It didn't take an hour. Twenty minutes later Peyton called Lily and Shay back into the office.

The hacker shot them both a shit-eating grin. "I'm too damned good for this world. I'm the king of all researchers. Omniscient, in practical terms."

Lily rolled her eyes.

Shay shrugged. "Show, don't tell, Peyton."

Peyton clapped his hands. "So, here's the deal. The egg was commissioned as a gift by Tsar Alexander III for his wife, Maria."

"Yeah, rich royal gives an expensive gift to his wife. That's not a shocking revelation. It's definitely low on the list of revelations granted by omniscience."

He grinned like he was Osiris catching a mouse. "Yeah, but did you know there were rumors that his wife Maria had an Oriceran heritage?"

Shay blinked. "No shit, really?"

Lily nodded. "Wonder how many royals had that kind of thing. Maybe that was why they were so obsessed with their bloodlines."

Peyton shrugged. "Don't know, but the thing is, her

husband died in 1894, and she lived until 1928, including through that little unpleasantness known as the Russian Revolution. There are more than a few rumors that some dark magic was involved in her lifespan, but the thing we care about at the moment is that she allegedly infused some sort of magical energy into the egg. Quite a lot. People who have tried to access the energy ended up...well, they had bad endings. To this day, allegedly no one knows how to access the energy of the egg."

Shay nodded. "Okay, now this is sounding more like my kind of job. So, I'm guessing they at least have some clue where it is, or *you* have some clue where it is. Otherwise, you wouldn't be so smug and happy."

He nodded. "It's Argentina, where all the bad white boys have gone to retire throughout the ages."

She smirked. "Maybe I'll get to kill a few Hitler clones while I'm down there."

Lily frowned. "What about the energy? And what exactly is a bad end?"

Shay pointed toward Lily. "Girl asks some good questions. Do you have good answers?"

Peyton rubbed the back of his neck. "Well, yeah, those are some good questions, and I have some answers, but um..."

"Spit it the fuck out already."

"They melted." Peyton shrugged.

"Huh?" Shay blinked.

"The people who tried to access the energy melted like those Nazis looking at the Ark in that old movie you made me watch last week."

Shay rolled her eyes. "Now you're disrespecting the classics."

"Just saying, there might be a few Nazi mummies down there in need of melting. It *is* Argentina, after all."

Lily shuddered. "Melted? That's harsh."

Peyton managed a smile. "Good news is, at least there are no demonic chickens involved. Bad news is that if you want the job, you're going to have fly out tonight, according to the offer."

Shay considered that. She normally wanted a little more background before she agreed to take on a job, but twenty million was a lot of money even by her standards.

Not like I can't bail if things go south.

"Dig some more," Shay ordered. "And pass anything you find along to me on the way. Book two seats on a supersonic flight. It'll probably still take a good six hours to get down there, and that gives you plenty of time to find some shit out." She shook her finger. "Make sure you get all the relevant info before I leave the airport down there. I don't want to end up a puddle. That's a pretty damned pathetic way to die."

Lily eyes widened, and she looked at Shay and Peyton.

Shay shrugged at the girl. "You don't have to come if you think it's too dangerous."

The girl shook her head. "And pass up my chance to maybe see melting Nazis?"

4

An hour later, Shay was walking among racks of firearms, grenades, knives, and gadgets in Warehouse Three. Regardless of what Peyton found out, she needed to go in with a standard complement of weapons. The egg might not melt them, but it wouldn't do them any good if someone shot them in the face before they got anywhere near it.

She pulled down several guns and knives and dropped them into a box.

Need more artifacts, so I don't have to rely on guns and the adamantine knives so much. If I had more artifacts, I probably could have beaten Yulia. Magic might be annoying, but it's still damned necessary.

Lily eyed the box. "I still don't quite understand how you get away with this."

"Get away with what?"

"Bringing all sorts of guns and grenades and stuff like that on planes. It seems like most of the time you take commercial."

Shay nodded. "Yeah, that's true."

Lily shook her head. "Yeah, I've only flown with you on a few private flights, but mostly commercial. How do you smuggle boxes of weapons past security and customs without ending up in some foreign dungeon? Even if you could explain away the guns, I doubt anyone allows people to fly with grenades in their luggage."

Shay winked. "It's all about knowing the right people and hacking the right systems in other situations." She shrugged. "It's really not a big deal. It helps if I'm with James on occasion, because they pretty much let him bring anything he wants legally, but most of the time, I'm not doing jobs with him. The thing is, if I'm flying a short distance, it's very easy to arrange a private plane, but there aren't a bunch of supersonic planes out there that I can easily charter for private trips. Doesn't matter that I've been..."

She frowned. Lily didn't know about her pre-tomb raider past and didn't need to know. It wasn't that Shay was ashamed. It was more that it'd unnecessarily complicate their relationship. She might not be James, but the last thing she needed was more complications in her relationships.

Shay forced a smile. "Let's just say I know how to get a thing or two through customs and security." She leaned over to start grabbing boxes of magazines. "Since you've been hiding in your tunnels lately, I don't even know if you still have what it takes."

The girl rolled her eyes and brushed some gray hair out of her eyes. "You make it sound like it's been months. It hasn't been that long."

"Just saying." The tomb raider moved past her and set the box down on a table. She pulled out a small 9mm and a magazine and handed it to Lily. "Prove it. A person-melting egg isn't a junior varsity mission."

Without hesitation, the teen slapped the magazine into the gun and readied the pistol. She marched across the room and aimed at a paper target down a shooting lane. Lily whipped up the pistol, took aim, and fired three times. She lowered the weapon and flipped the safety on, a smirk on her face.

Shay pressed a button, and the hanging target slid toward the pair. When it arrived, there was a tight center-mass cluster of hits.

She nodded. "Well, all right then. You have always been a natural."

Lily smirked and handed Shay the gun, grip-first. "Was that why you decided to train me?"

The tomb raider shrugged. "Maybe I just see a little of myself in you." She walked back over to the other side of the room, ejected the magazine, and placed the gun in the box. "That, and you can sometimes see the future. It's just a little incentive." She pressed her thumb and finger together. "Teensy little bit."

The teen followed her. "Going to get some grenades, too?"

"Never know when one might come in handy, and I'd rather say, 'Darn, didn't need it' than 'Shit, I really wish I had a grenade right now.'" Shay's phone rang. "What's up, Peyton?"

"I've got the background info you need," he answered.

"At least enough to not get melted. I figured telling you now might make your flight more comfortable."

Shay snorted. "Yeah, not getting melted is pretty high on my list of important shit."

"I've got to give you credit. We're not even at the airport yet. I thought it'd take you a little while to hack your way around to it."

"I'm not a one-trick pony. This is where I got to demonstrate my fine bargaining skills."

"What do you mean? What bargaining skills?"

Peyton chuckled. "In the course of doing my normal thing for you I come across a lot of information on artifacts, but most of it is low- or mid-range garbage. Basically, stuff you wouldn't get out of bed to recover but might pick up if it were on the ground and you had nothing better to do."

"Okay, I get that, what's that have to do with me not getting melted and your bargaining skills?"

Peyton laughed. "Well, just because *you* don't care doesn't mean other people don't care. So, I traded some info on an artifact you don't give a crap about to get information on an artifact you care about, namely the egg and its dangers, with someone on the dark web."

Shay nodded toward the box and walked over to her grenade shelf. Lily picked up the box and followed her, curiosity in her gray eyes.

The hacker sighed. "Anyway, we've got one of those classic good news-slash-bad news situations."

The tomb raider started grabbing grenades from the shelf to set in the box. "Give me the good news first. I always like to end on a pissy note."

"Don't I know it! Good news is you should be able to get the egg without melting. It was moved to Argentina without teleportation, so that proves it's possible."

"Now give me the bad news."

"Yeah, well, the only people who can handle the egg directly are those with equally strong magic."

Shay tossed a sonic grenade into the box and frowned at her phone. "You just told me I could handle it without melting. Unless I somehow managed to be a witch or Oriceran all these years without knowing it, I don't think I'm gonna suddenly manifest strong magic."

"Sure, sure. But you can still move it. From what I've been told, it wasn't a wizard who last moved it, so you just need to figure out how. What I've found out is that you have to be prepared to grab the egg, but not with your bare hands or a piece of cloth, or anything like that."

The tomb raider scoffed. "So I can handle it, as long I just don't touch it directly or indirectly."

"Yeah, that's about it. Hope you have some ideas, but like I said, we at least know it's possible."

Shay chuckled. "I've got a few ideas I'll try for twenty million. Transmit all the relevant location data to me when you get a chance. I'm gonna finish arming up here and then head to the airport with Lily."

A cat yowled in the background on Peyton's end and a loud crash followed.

Shay snickered. "I don't even want to know what the hell is going on. Talk to you later."

Peyton mumbled something under his breath as she hung up.

Lily lifted the box and shrugged. "Problems?"

"How much do you know about handling dangerous artifacts?"

She shrugged. "A little. My father showed me a few things, but not going to lie and say I'm an expert."

Shay nodded. "Let's pack this gear up in a few of my special boxes for the airport. We'll make a stop before we hit it."

"Where's that?"

The tomb raider grinned. "A place where I can show you a few more things about handling artifacts. There's just one more thing I need to grab here first."

Lily peered around the large open space of the main room of Warehouse Five with a frown on her face. "This looks a lot like Warehouse Three. I mean, you've got a bunch of racks of stuff, and it just looks like random crap, at that." She pointed to a velvet painting of a young Drake from twenty years prior when he was still in his prime. "Talk about random. I thought you said this was some big artifact warehouse, not the world's lamest garbage dump."

Shay laughed. "Most of that random stuff is just about confusing people. Almost all of it is random junk that was here, or that I bought just to mess with people if they found this place. Artifacts aren't always obvious, so it helps keep people on their toes."

Lily looked back and forth. "But there's lots of magic in this place. Even some on the racks."

"Yeah. I've got a few minor artifacts here and there as chaff, but none of the good stuff. Sure, it won't fool an

Oriceran or a wizard, but the typical idiot hitman wouldn't get any of the good artifacts even if he got in here. Not that that would ever happen, but it always helps to have multiple lines of defense."

"So, where's the real stuff, then?"

"This is where it gets cool." Shay marched over to a wall in the corner and pressed her palm against the middle. A small portion of the wall retracted to reveal a retinal scanner. She leaned in, and after the scan, another small silver panel revealed itself.

"Got enough locks?"

Shay shook her head. "Probably not. I've thought about getting magical locks on here, too."

The tomb raider placed her thumb on the silver panel and waited for the telltale burn of a DNA scan.

She grinned. "You're getting to see something cool and new. I remodeled some of this lately. Let me tell you, that's not easy when you have to bring in a bunch of people blindfolded and use artifacts to block their ability to be traced. Not cheap either."

The entire wall slid open to reveal two joysticks, a keyboard, and a couple of displays set in a black console at waist level. Thick plexiglass separated the rest of the vast and dark hidden chamber from the main warehouse.

"Welcome to my artifact vault." Shay grinned. "Bulletproof glass. Also has a few enchantments on it to take minor spells and help disrupt magical tracking. Guess it's a good thing I'm about to earn twenty million. Gonna need to pay for all the upgrades I just did for this place. The thing is almost completely automated now."

Lily looked at Shay. "It wasn't before?"

"Nope. I just had the vault and stuff sitting inside it on shelves."

Lily furrowed her brow. "Why did you automate it then?"

Shay shrugged a single shoulder. "Here's a little test. Why do *you* think I might have automated it?"

"I'm guessing it's not just because you're lazy."

The tomb raider snorted. "Nope."

The Gray Elf teen stepped toward the plexiglass and tapped it with her index finger. "My father told me that a lot of people don't get that magical artifacts aren't like technology. A lot of them will respond to you, and maybe respond badly if you're using them for something you shouldn't be."

"Yeah, Tubal-Cain has gone on about that several times to me. After about the fiftieth time he told me that, I bought a clue and decided that I don't know if some asshole artifact is judging me, so the less I'm handling things directly, the better. Don't want to get turned into a bird or something one day." Shay nodded toward the arti-fact vault. "So I had this system created. Better safe than melted or winged." She marched over to the keyboard. "By the way, just to make it clear, you can't tell *anyone* about this place. Peyton knows something like it exists, but he has no idea where. I'd strongly prefer he not know."

Lily blinked a few times and stepped toward the plexi-glass. "And I thought *I* had trust issues. You already threated to kill me over Warehouse Two's location, so… what, you'll kill me two and half times as much if I rat out this place's location?"

"Something like that." The tomb raider nodded. "This is

a whole different level of secret. This is the kind of stuff that very dangerous people would kill everyone in your tunnels over, so it's as much for your own safety as mine." She tapped in some commands on the keyboard. An automated arm descended from the ceiling and whizzed into the dark distance. About thirty seconds later, it reappeared with a long, curved sword in a scabbard—Shay's enchanted Masamune *tachi.*

Lily nodded. "So this is where you've been keeping it instead of Warehouse Three."

"Yep. Had to get a new scabbard, though, because my boyfriend broke my old one on a little field trip to Oriceran. Fortunately, it wasn't magic, so I was only seriously pissed instead of completely pissed. It was damned nice, though. I still yelled at him about it."

"Well, when you date the Scourge of Harriken you have to expect that kind of thing." The teen shrugged.

"Yeah, true enough." Shay smirked and entered a few more commands. A window opened in the bottom of the plexiglass, and she reached into it and grabbed the scabbard. She handed it to Lily.

"I don't keep my adamantine knives or my lockpick at Warehouse Five, but most other shit I do." More commands followed. "Now if we're lucky, and the egg is the size we expect it to be, I've got a solution that should involve no melting."

Again, the arm whirred into the darkness.

Lily peered into the glass. "An artifact solution to a dangerous artifact? Isn't that doubling-down on risk?"

"Nope. It's more about managing risk."

The arm brought back what appeared to be a simple

wooden lidded box. No writing or decoration adorned it. You might find it anywhere in the world.

An opening reappeared in the plexiglass, and Shay grabbed the box. "I got this on a quick but nasty tomb raid for a client who unfortunately kicked the bucket before he could pay me. I took this as my payment."

"What's it do?"

"It's supposed to be able to protect whatever is held inside of it. I'm just hoping the egg will fit."

Lily eyed the box. "Supposed to? You've never tested it?"

Shay shrugged and handed the girl the box. "I did some low-level tests. Put an artifact in there and shot it. It didn't dent, but it's not like I've had a chance to test it against flesh-melting magic. That doesn't come up all that often even in my line of work."

She winked. "If you get anything out of my training, you should learn that most of these things we find out as we go. That's just kind of what it means to be a tomb raider."

5

Static crackled in Shay's earpiece.

Lily frowned and tapped at hers. "Can you hear Peyton?"

Shay shook her head. "Nope." She nodded at the phone built into the SUV's console. "I haven't even been able to get a satellite signal for the last hour." She pulled out her earpiece. "Might as well just turn it off for now. It's useless."

Everything from their flight to the trip to their target location had gone well, so Shay wasn't surprised that something had finally gone wrong. It didn't matter. She had all the data she needed to complete the tomb raid already downloaded to her phone. She'd half-expected something like this to happen.

Lily glanced at Shay. "Is that why you kept sticking your arm out the window? To check your satellite phone reception?"

"Yep. Point is, we have line-of-sight to the sky from this

road. If I can't get a signal, that means general interference and not just some weird magnetic field or something."

Lily furrowed her brow. "Jammer?"

Shay shook her head. "Don't think so, but there isn't a magical storm or anything, so it's natural, or magically natural. You sense anything? See anything?"

The girl shrugged. "Nothing in particular, and the only thing I see in our future is more driving."

Shay snickered. "Don't have to be clairvoyant to guess that." She shrugged. "But it doesn't matter. The interference will clear up once we get out of the mountains, and it's not like Peyton can hack anything up here to help us. Drones are often not all that great in small caves. If anything, this might be a good thing."

Lily laughed. "How is a bunch of interference a good thing? Even if he couldn't help us with the cave, he could watch the outside for us."

"Sure, but among other things, if *we* can't have someone watch the outside with a drone, it means no one else can either. It also means no one can sneak up a drone with rockets to try to blow our asses up."

"Has that happened to you?"

Shay nodded. "Yes. It's really fucking annoying. A little bit of everything has happened to me on this job. Remind me to tell you someday how I think I doomed Russia to a supernatural empress in the future."

"Uh, okay, then. I think I'll just stop talking for now."

The tomb raider grinned.

Lily gave her a quick nod and fell into silence, her gray eyes locked on the passenger-side window.

The SUV continued to rattle along the snow-covered

dirt road on their way up the back of the Argentinian mountain called *Cerro Catedral*. The vehicle could take them a good part of the way, and then more than a little hiking through the snow would be necessary.

Their heavy coats would help, but fortunately, from what Peyton's information indicated, they wouldn't have to do any true mountain-climbing versus glorified hiking. Ice-climbing wasn't something Shay'd had a lot of experience with.

Maybe I should start practicing that. Hate to miss out an artifact because I can't get to it.

Lily stared out at the white wonderland. "Maybe it's lame considering I'm part elf and can see the future, but it's really weirding me out that it's winter here when it's summer back home. It's messing with my brain. It just feels so wrong."

Shay chuckled. "That's how the raids get you. It's not the strange and exotic that breaks your brain when you see some weird ghost or bunyip or whatever. Those are so out there that it's easy to compartmentalize. It's just another monster on the checklist of problems to get through, something you know you won't see again once you get home. But the other stuff—time zones, climate differences, hemispheres, different languages—it's unsettling, but not alien. So it stays with you; it lingers and seeps into your soul." She shook her head. "But it's all the kind of crap you need to get used to as a tomb raider. It'd be nice if everything could just be hidden under a Walmart in Illinois, but it's rare that I don't have to leave the country for a tomb raid."

"You get to go and see the world, at least. Maybe that's

why I like the idea so much. I like my friends and LA, but there's a whole world out there. Heck, there are a couple of whole worlds out there, and I've barely even seen any of mine."

Shay grinned.

Not just a couple of worlds, kid.

"True enough," Shay agreed. "Half the time that world is trying to kill me, but at least I get to see it. Not a bad life, as long as you understand you'll never be safe."

"Not like my life in LA is safe." Lily frowned. "But when you think about it, this is kind of more like the Walmart situation than some weird ancient tomb in Egypt."

Shay glanced her way. "How do you figure? We're grabbing this thing out of an allegedly hidden part of a cave."

"But it's not a remote mountain in the middle of nowhere. From what Peyton sent us, this place is a ski resort. We're not that far from a bunch of tourists and South American ski bunnies. If they got lost on the mountain, they could almost end up in the cave."

Shay nodded. "True enough. What's the problem? You look a little annoyed by that. Not exotic enough for your tourist desires?"

"Not annoyed, just confused." Lily shook her head. "I don't get why no one has found the artifact. Even if they couldn't handle it, you figure the government would have sealed off the cave with a big warning sign—Caution, flesh-melting egg inside. That kind of thing. Maybe bomb it closed or something. You know, typical government overreaction stuff."

Shay shrugged. "Who knows? There might be a glamour on the cave, so unless you know exactly what you're looking for, you won't find it. I've run into that kind of thing a lot. Or it's just the right time of year for us to find it. Sometimes it's easy to hide things in plain sight." She turned off the main road into a thicket of tall and dense trees. "I'm less worried about a few wayward ski assholes than I am competition. From the info Peyton sent along, other tomb raiders are targeting this place."

"That was why we had to leave right away?"

"Yep. Maybe I should have told you that before I told you to come along."

Lily shook her head. "I can't run away every time there's a little danger, and other tomb raiders are less scary than invisible cursed sword ghosts or Yulia." She nodded, determination on her face. "I can do this. I need to get more experience, and the only way to do that is to go with you on jobs."

Shay frowned a little. She was enjoying training Lily, but even as helpful as it was, the girl was supposed to be getting something out of it, too. Maybe it was time to push her a little and make her think about her future more.

"With your share of this," Shay offered, "you can probably set your friends up somewhere other than those tunnels, you know. I've already given you some decent money. You don't have to keep doing that magical Artful Dodger shit."

"Yeah, I know. I've been talking with Harry about that." Lily laughed. "The funny thing is, now that I'm bringing money in, we're not sure what to do with it. We've gotten so used to living the way we have that it's hard to adjust. We don't have to scavenge for food, but we're also not sure about the idea of leaving the tunnels.

Funny how that works. We know them, and feel safe there in a way that we wouldn't feel safe in apartments on the surface."

Shay frowned and did a quick mirror check. Nothing but snow and trees. "I get it. It's hard to leave your old life behind, even if you should."

"Did you leave an old life behind?"

"Not like I've always been a tomb raider."

Lily stared at her for a moment. "And what did you do before you were a tomb raider?"

Shay shook her head. "I'll tell you someday when I feel like it, but today isn't that day. Today, we just concentrate on not getting melted."

The tomb raider and her trainee fell silent, lost in their thoughts of the past.

Shay tromped up the hill through the snow. They might not be having to crack out pitons and rope, but waist-high snow wasn't exactly fun to trudge through. Their vehicle was a distant black bump down the side of the mountain.

Lily groaned. "If this is reminding me of anything, it's that I'm a true Southern Californian."

The tomb raider laughed. "I'm still not sure which annoys me more, being very cold or very hot. I'll say one thing, though. It's not as bad as Antarctica, and I'm not just talking about that damned witch."

"Just saying, maybe next time you can take a nice tomb raiding job in Hawaii or the Bahamas."

"I'll keep that in mind."

A dark opening loomed several hundred yards above them.

Shay grinned. "We're almost there." She patted Lily's backpack. The box rested inside. "The trick will just be getting it into the box, and then we're home-free, and will be much, much richer."

"I'm not touching it. Just so you know."

"Neither of us are. Hard to spend money when we're dead."

Shay hissed when a stiff wind coated them with snow. "At least in the cave, there won't be as much wind."

The minutes passed as the snow crunched underneath their boots until they stood at the entrance of a surprisingly smooth and warm cave. Icicles hung from the entrance, but the snow and ice extended only a few feet inside.

Lily squinted and pointed to several silver pools littering the front of the cave. "What the heck are those? Mercury?"

Shay moved over toward one of the pools and kicked a pebble into it. The pebble sank without producing any ripples. A chill ran through her body, and it wasn't from the cold wind.

The tomb raider clucked her tongue. "Poor bastards."

"Huh?"

Shay pointed to the nearest pool. "Too thick to be mercury, and it's not warm enough to be melted silver or anything like that. I'm pretty sure those are what's left over from some of the other people who tried to take the egg."

Lily grimaced. "At least we know we're on the right track."

"That we do." Shay took a single step forward and frowned. The hair on the back of her neck stood up, and she looked over her shoulder. "Something's not right. Damn it."

Lily looked behind her. "What? I don't see anything but trees and snow." She shook her head. "And I'm not sensing anything. Can't see the future right now."

The tomb raider fished binoculars out of her backpack and started scanning the area. "I trust my instincts. I know when I'm being watched."

"Wait, like a premonition? You've never mentioned that before."

Shay shook her head and continued to scan. "Nothing like. It's just experience. Probably just keying in on some subtle sense thing." A flash caught her attention, and she jerked her head in that direction. Two men in parkas stood in the trees about a half-mile away. One had binoculars to his eyes.

She adjusted her binoculars. She couldn't make out a lot of fine details, but she did recognize the emblem on their coats.

"The assholes even have custom coats. You've got to be kidding me. Fucking arrogant jerks."

Lily frowned. "Who are you talking about?"

"Hollingsworth Retrieval Specialists. They are tomb raiders based out of England. They aren't completely ruthless murderers, I'll give them that, but they also don't know when to give up. The assholes probably thought they could just wait over there and swoop in and take the egg." Shay lowered her binoculars and looked at Lily. "Seeing anything yet?"

The girl shook her head. "No visions."

Shay let out a dark chuckle. "Maybe fifteen minutes from now we're cute little silver pools, too." She stuffed the binoculars into her backpack. "Time to go make the future happen."

"What about the English guys?"

Shay shrugged. "If they want to come and actually play, then we'll worry about them. For now, we've got an egg to find."

Twenty minutes into the cave, it had grown warm enough that Shay wanted to take off her coat. She wasn't sure if it was a geothermal or magical effect but decided a little unzipping and unbuttoning would be enough. It'd give her better access to her weapons anyway.

Their wrist lights cut into the darkness as they moved deeper into the cave, but thus far, the closest thing to exciting they'd encountered was some moss.

That is, until the cave shook and gave a deep rumble.

"That's not good," Lily observed. "Is this mountain a volcano?"

"Beats me." Shay shrugged. "It doesn't matter. Even *I* don't have such bad luck that it'd erupt the second I show up. Let's just find it and get the hell out of here, then we won't have to worry. Visions yet?"

Lily shook her head. "Still nothing." She frowned. "Damn it. I'm sorry."

"Hey, don't beat yourself up over it. Most of my jobs,

the only thing I have to go on is background data that Peyton or I dug up."

A couple more minutes brought to them a fork, the round tunnels just as unnaturally smooth as the rest of the cave. Shay doubted this was a natural cave, but she didn't care about magical civil engineering projects, just the egg they were designed to protect.

A stronger tremor shook the cave.

Shay gritted her teeth. "Any clues?"

Lily pointed to the left fork. "It's that way."

"Nice. That simplifies things." Shay jogged down the tunnel.

Lily hurried after her.

Shay didn't want to believe her eyes as their lights illuminated a dead end. She frowned.

"You sure it was this way?"

Lily nodded and pointed at the wall. "That's magical."

The tomb raider hurried over to the wall and looked it over. "Well, it looks like everything else in here. Probably stupid to touch it, but here we go."

Shay swallowed, reached out, and poked the wall. Her finger went right through.

"What the hell?" Further probing proved her entire hand could go through, as could her arm. She grinned at Lily. "It's just an illusion. That's the magic you're sensing."

Shay shrugged and stepped through the wall. A cavern larger than any of the tunnels in the cave was on the other side. The target of their quest, an ornate jeweled egg, sat in the center of a small stone platform with a dip in the center. Two large silver pools lay on either side, and there was a smaller pool in the corner.

Lily appeared through the wall. "Great, more melted people. That's really making me feel good."

Shay frowned and pointed at the smaller pool. "But why is *that* there? No one could touch the egg from that far away."

She headed toward the pool with Lily close behind.

Another tremor rocked the cave and the pools shook, moving a few inches.

"Guess that answers that." She stared at the egg. "But wait. There were pools at the entrance to the cave. No way they slid all the way back there."

Lily pulled the protective box out of her backpack. "Why don't we get the egg and run away, so we don't have to find out the answers? The platform's magical, too. It might call the egg back after a while if no one has it."

"Maybe. I think we'll go with your grabbing and running idea for now." Shay stepped toward the egg and stopped about a yard away. "Just have to figure out how to get it in the box."

The teen removed the lid and moved toward it. "Maybe if I knock it with the lid."

Shay's heart rate kicked up. "No," she snapped. She took a deep breath. "Pretty sure if you're touching it, even through something else, you'll end up a pool. I've grown attached to you, kid. Don't melt yourself."

The cavern shuddered wildly, and the egg fell from the platform and hit the floor.

The tomb raider winced, half-expecting it to explode in a wave of powerful magic, but instead, it rolled along the floor toward the fake wall.

"Get it," Shay shouted, her heart galloping.

Lily leaped in front of it and slammed the box into its path, her hand still on the bottom. The lid skittered across the dirt, dust, and rocks on the cave floor. The egg rolled straight toward it. A foot, then six inches, then an inch.

"Let go, Lily."

The girl yelped and released her grip on the box. The egg rolled inside, the force of the collision knocking the box upright.

They both stared down at the box that now contained the deadly artifact, then they exchanged glances.

Shay shrugged. "Sometimes you just get lucky." She grabbed the lid from the ground and knelt by the box.

Lily hissed and shook her head.

Shay silenced her with a raised palm. "If this is gonna work, I should be able to put this on without melting."

The girl nodded. "That's a big *if.*"

"See anything? A little future insight would be nice about now."

Lily sighed and shook her head.

Shay swallowed and slowly lowered the lid toward the box, her heart thundering. She was placing a lot of faith in a box she'd only tested against a few types of physical and magical damage. Her hand inched down, and she took a deep breath.

Fuck, James. I chewed you out about your dumbass pay-per-view stunt, but here I am risking melting.

"Fuck it!" Shay screamed and slammed the lid down.

She stared at Lily, and the girl stared back. Neither dared move or breathe. The seconds ticked by until Shay realized something more than a little important. She hadn't melted. At least she thought she hadn't.

The tomb raider grabbed the box and lifted it. "Did I melt?"

Lily shook her head. "You don't look like you melted."

Shay laughed. She set the box down and then pulled off her backpack so she could put the box in the top of it before zipping it shut.

"Always a good day when you don't melt."

Lily rolled her eyes. "Yeah, that's what I say every night before I go to sleep."

"Now let's get the hell out of here."

The two stepped through the illusionary wall, right into a pack of six large men in parkas.

Shay groaned. "They came into the cave?"

One of the men grinned. "Give us the egg, and there won't be any trouble."

Another tremor shook the cave.

None of the men had guns out, which killed Shay's immediate instinct to gun them all down.

These assholes do a lot of work for the British government, and if I waste them in front of Lily, I might be pushing her down the path I was on. I should try to beat their asses down without killing them, as long as they don't push me too far.

Shay shook her head. "Not gonna happen, assholes. Don't make this difficult. No one has to get hurt."

The man frowned and looked at Lily. "You brought a kid? What the hell?"

"I'm a kid who can kick your ass," the girl spat back.

When the cave shook again, Shay sprang forward and delivered a quick roundhouse kick to the nearest tomb raider. His head snapped back, and he slammed into the wall.

Two of the other men grabbed for the tomb raider, and she jumped backward and spun to deliver an elbow to the face of one of the men before kicking another man into the wall.

"Bloody hell," one of three remaining men shouted. He yanked a contact Taser out of a pocket.

Lily slapped it out of his hand, grabbed it with her other hand before it hit the ground, and planted it in his neck. He twitched and jerked as the Taser crackled.

"Come on," Shay shouted. She sprinted forward, and Lily rushed after her.

The two conscious tomb raiders didn't pursue them. Instead, they knelt to check on their fallen friends.

You care more about your friends than the artifact. You're all right. Too bad we had to beat your asses.

She was glad to escape. The bulky parkas their opponents were wearing might not be armor, but they did deny Shay access to body targets that would have made taking them down in a non-lethal manner easier.

Not killing people is a lot fucking harder than just killing them.

Shay and Lily continued charging for the cave entrance. The pair just needed to get to their vehicle.

The cave started getting lighter even as it shook. They were close to the entrance, and no one was closing on them from the rear.

Looks like we're home free.

The tomb raider and her protégé ran past the silver pools and out of the cave. Two steps out of the cave, a large group of men rushed at them from either side of the cave entrance.

"Shit," Shay hissed.

The deep snow slowed Shay's pivot, and one of the men slammed into her. Both went to the ground, but a quick throat punch had the man gasping and rolling off her.

"It's free," one of the men shouted, and pointed.

Shay jerked her head that way. Her zipper had come undone, and the box had fallen out. The lid was askew, and the egg lay loose in the snow.

The Hollingsworth tomb raider charged through the snow, a huge grin on his face.

"Don't touch it," one of the other men shouted.

The idiot ignored them and snatched up the egg with his gloved hands. He grinned and held it above him like a trophy. "Yeah, bonus time."

His good mood lasted all of two seconds. He twitched and screamed. Argent lines shot all over his skin and clothes in an instant, and a moment later, a mass of thick silver liquid roughly in the shape of a man hung in the air where the tomb raider had once stood.

Shay blinked, the horror of seeing a man melt piercing even her jaded heart.

The egg fell toward the ground, and a blur ran past her. Lily, protective box in hand, jumped underneath the egg, catching it in the box.

She stared at it, panting. No one else said a word. The other Hollingsworth tomb raiders continued to stare at the silver pool in the snow that had once been their teammate.

The teen stood slowly and grabbed the lid off the ground. She set it back on the box and backed away from the men.

One of the Hollingsworth men looked up at Shay and shook his head. "Just go already. Shit."

Shay gave him a quick nod and jogged off with Lily toward the SUV at the bottom of the incline. After about fifty yards, she glanced over her shoulder. The men hadn't moved.

She could understand what they were feeling, even if they were enemies.

That could have been Lily.

6

Spending hours holding a box containing a human-liquifying artifact didn't do wonders for Shay's nerves. Even a stone-cold tomb raider could be rattled, and seeing a man taken out in a moment had accomplished just that.

Pain suffused her neck and shoulders, and she hadn't spoken much to Lily on the plane back or on the ride back to the tunnels.

It wasn't that hard. Both of them were exhausted from the travel and the tomb raid, and neither wanted to spend time chatting about watching a man being melted by an artifact.

At least it'll be a good payday. She should seriously think about moving her friends out of those tunnels.

Shay even allowed herself a long nap on the flight back, while Lily decided to take in the latest Caleb Rodriguez film. She almost wanted to laugh. There was something bizarre about going on a dangerous tomb raid just to get on a plane and watch a movie about a fictional tomb raider.

Maybe by watching the movie, she could put what had happened out of her mind. In the end, Caleb always gets the artifact, and the bad guys get what was coming to them.

Are those Hollingsworth assholes the bad guys? I didn't have any more right to that egg than they did, and they didn't go out of their way to kill us. They could have pulled guns and not a Taser. Maybe the good guy died, and the bad girl got away with the loot.

The tomb raider stopped her car when she and Lily arrived at one of the ten-foot-diameter pipes leading into the nuclear shelter and blew out a breath. "I got you home in one piece. You all right? I know that was a harder one than usual."

Lily shrugged. "Not saying I wasn't spooked, but I'll be okay. Maybe it's a bitch thing to say, but it's not like I knew the guy, and it's not the first person I've seen killed."

Shay chuckled. "True enough."

The teen glanced into the back seat. They'd secured the box and the lid in the back. "I can't help but wonder…"

"Wonder what?"

Lily sighed. "What do you even do with something like that? It's kind of elaborate if it's just about killing people."

Shay shrugged. "Good question. I honestly don't know. I'm guessing someone wants the power stored in that thing. For what? Your guess is as good as mine. Maybe they want to power something even freakier."

Lily shook her head. "You told me before, and my dad mentioned to me how artifacts can respond to what people want to do with them. Like, you have to be careful with how you use them. Not use them for the wrong stuff."

"Yeah. What about it?"

Lily nodded toward the box. "Maybe that's the end result of using something for evil. Maybe they used it all for the wrong stuff, and now it's an egg of evil."

Shay shrugged. "Who knows? I don't know if the tsar's wife was evil, or maybe she was trying to prepare something for revenge. Considering what happened I wouldn't be surprised, nor would I blame her."

Lily sighed and opened the door. "I need a little time to process everything. I probably won't stop by for a while."

"It's okay. Take all the time you need. You know where to find me." Shay forced a grin. "And I'm sure Harry's eager to see you and know you didn't get scratched."

The teen's cheeks reddened, and she stepped out of the car. "Um, yeah, I'm sure he is."

"Okay, then, see you around. It was good to have you on the job again. Next time, I'll try to take us somewhere tropical." The tomb raider stared at the girl for a moment.

Lily gave her a sad smile, and with a final wave, she marched toward the pipe.

Should have offered to let her stay in the warehouse. After the shit I made her see, it's the least I can do. But now that she's here, there's no way she's gonna want to leave. I'm still new in her life, not like all these kids who have had her back for years.

Maybe that was some harsh shit, but it's a good thing. She needs to see the kinds of dangers you might run into during a tomb raid. It's not just invisible ghosts and witches. Some things are far freakier, and the earlier she learns that, the better.

Shay took a deep breath and pulled the car back onto the road. Twenty million dollars was a lot of money. All she needed to do was hand over the artifact, and she'd score her biggest payday yet.

She could even have Peyton contact the buyer and demand additional money for the protection box unless the client somehow had their own method for safely containing the egg. Assuming a client wasn't an idiot wasn't usually a good plan. Lots of rich fools paid a lot of money for artifacts they couldn't hope to understand or control.

Wonder if those Hollingsworth guys had a plan. The other guys seemed to get that they shouldn't touch it, but no one had anything that looked like an artifact. Were they just banking on me *having a plan?*

She shook her head. It didn't matter. Even if her time away from professional killing and her exposure to Alison and James had dulled her old ruthlessness, she didn't have the time or energy to worry about competing tomb raiders. If the men had demonstrated any lethal intent at all, she would have killed them without hesitation. She wasn't even sure if she'd have spared their lives if Lily hadn't been there with her.

Is it so much worse to get melted than have your throat cut or be shot? Dead is dead, in the end.

After a few seconds, Shay barked out a laugh. No. Being melted was definitely worse than being shot.

For the moment, she needed to just get the damned artifact contained. All her efforts at upgrading Warehouse Five seemed prescient now. The box containing the deadly egg had an appointment with her automated storage vault.

She'd driven twenty miles brooding about the artifact when her phone rang with a call from Peyton.

Shay answered it on speakerphone. "I just got done dropping Lily off. She's a little spooked with how things went down, but she'll be okay."

Peyton sighed. "I want to apologize again."

Shay snorted. "It's not your fault."

"I feel like crap that those guys got the drop on you. Not only did I let tomb raiders jump you, but I also let Hollingsworth of all people jump you." He groaned.

"So? Until someone invents a super-drone that can't be jammed, there will be times you won't be able to have my back. We both need to plan for that. Maybe someday we'll get lucky and find a magical cell phone, but for now, we have to work with what we've got. When you can help me, you can help me, and when you can't, you can't. Anyway, it's not like they won. We got away with the egg. And they lost a guy." Shay allowed a little hope to creep into her voice. "The point is, I didn't get hurt, Lily didn't get hurt, and I got the artifact. That's a win however you want to look at it."

Peyton's swallowing was audible over the line.

Shay frowned. "Why are you so nervous?"

"How do you know I'm nervous?" Tension pitched his voice higher.

The tomb raider rolled her eyes. Peyton was great at many things, but she doubted he'd ever cultivate the true hardness necessary for the world they inhabited.

"You sound nervous, Peyton. You don't have a poker face or a poker voice." Shay did a quick mirror check, more paranoid than normal because of the artifact in a box in her backseat. "Which means you have bad news to deliver to me, and not just annoying shit. When it's that kind of thing, you just tell some stupid joke. So, someone's got you seriously spooked?" The tomb raider frowned. "Is James telling you to keep something from me again?"

"I wish it were just that, but no, that's not it."

"Then what?"

Peyton took a deep breath. "Correk just called me."

"What the hell? He called you directly?"

"Yeah. He said he couldn't get you, and he told me to tell you when I got in touch with you that he wants to meet at the Leanan Sídhe *now*, and he said to bring the egg. He specifically said, 'Tell her to bring the Necessaire Egg.' He also kind of threatened us. Said there would be consequences if you didn't."

Shay gritted her teeth. "How the hell did he know about the egg? I didn't even have any missed calls from him."

"Well, he is a pretty powerful elf. I'm guessing he used a spell rather than a phone. I don't know. Is this really a guy you can risk pissing off?"

The steering wheel creaked under her tightening grip. "Fuck it. Fuck *him*."

"Huh?"

Shay accelerated. A little speeding wouldn't hurt now.

"I don't care if he's Correk. I've been thinking a lot about that egg, and how I wanted to handle it."

"I thought you said you had a system set up at Warehouse Five to handle it."

"That's not what I mean. After what I saw, no one should get their hands on this thing, so I'm gonna put it somewhere that's safe. And, yeah, that's Warehouse Five, and not in the hands of some Light Elf with delusions of fucking grandeur about how he's the magical FBI for the whole damned world."

"That sounds good and all," Peyton began, "but can't he magically track it or something? You've done a good job of hiding the warehouse from me, but I rely on technology, not magic."

Shay changed lanes and zoomed past a Currus. The magical autonomous taxis always vaguely annoyed her.

I'm too much of a control freak to give up my control to some spell.

"Don't worry about Correk tracking shit," Shay explained. "I recently upgraded Warehouse Five, including paying for serious magical scrying protection. Half the reason I was so interested in this job was that I spent a lot of money on those upgrades, both technological and magical."

"Okay, fair enough. What about the client, and the twenty million? If anything, it sounds like you need it more than you normally do."

The tomb raider snorted. "Fuck the client. Nothing good will come of anyone having this thing. I'm not letting this shit back into circulation, even if I piss off Correk and the client."

"I can understand that." Peyton blew out a breath. "You're going to take a hit to your rep, though, and what should I tell the client?"

"You tell the client we lost it. I'll survive the hit to my rep. It's not the first time Aletheia has failed, and I'm guessing if what happened to the Hollingsworth guy gets out, a lot of people won't even want to try to find the egg."

The hacker whistled. "I'm surprised."

"By what?"

"It's just hard to figure you out sometimes. I think we're good friends, but someone makes a casual joke, and you pull out your gun. Then I think I don't know you at all."

Shay snorted. "A few pointed reminders never hurt anyone."

"Sure. It's just interesting to see there's a line that you won't cross, even for twenty million dollars. I don't know if the Shay I originally worked for would have cared."

"Spare me the psychoanalysis, Peyton. You don't know as much about me as you think. But who the hell knows? Maybe there are more than a few lines that I won't cross now."

An hour later, Shay sat with her arms crossed across from Correk and the Professor. The latter wore a soft smile as he sipped at his beer. She wasn't sure if he was leaving the anger to his Light Elf friend or if he didn't care as much.

Correk shook his head. "Did you just say what I think you said? I'm trying to give you the benefit of the doubt. Maybe it's jet lag, and you're confused. That has to be the explanation."

No, you didn't just go there, elf. It's time to remind you just who the hell I am.

Shay snorted. "Unless you're deaf, then yeah. You can't have the egg. I don't give a shit if you're the Fixer. In case you forgot, I agreed to share information with you, and I'll recover artifacts for you if you pay me, but you don't tell me what to do. I *don't* work for you. I only fucking work for me."

Correk scrubbed a hand over his face. The Light Elf grimaced so hard he looked like he was in pain. "This isn't about trying to order you around, Miz Carson. It's about the danger associated with that artifact. It needs to be in good hands for your personal safety and the safety of everyone else."

The Professor glanced at the two but said nothing. He took another small sip of his beer and offered her a wry smile.

Shay scoffed. "I thought I'd already proven it to you, but apparently you need a reminder. I'm not a fucking idiot, Correk. I know how dangerous it is. I've witnessed it first-hand. Poof, insta-pool."

He frowned. "Then why not make sure it's in safe hands?"

"Because it already is."

"Whose?"

Shay narrowed her eyes. "Mine."

The Fixer blinked. "Wait. You didn't sell it?" More than a little surprise colored his voice.

So much for trust, you arrogant asshole.

The tomb raider glared at him with so much anger she was surprised he didn't wither and melt. She concentrated on the idea as if she could bring a lethal gaze into existence through sheer force of will. Unfortunately, the Light Elf didn't melt.

The Professor let out a loud laugh. A good swill of beer followed, and he shook his head, looking amused and not a bit angry or confused.

He shrugged. "I'm sorry, old friend, but I think Miz Carson answered your question."

Correk stared at the Professor like he'd lost his mind. "You can't possibly think it's okay?"

"Aye, I do. I think the egg stays with Miz Carson. For now. Some enemies are not worth making." He winked.

"Is this about James Brownstone?"

The Professor shook his head and nodded at Shay. "Nope, it's about Miz Carson. She's just as lethal and apt to…make a point with those who have wronged her."

At least someone at this table understands I'm not to be fucked with.

Correk rubbed the bridge of his nose. "This isn't a game. This is more serious than you can possibly imagine."

Shay tried to put even more irritation into her look. "No one fucking said it was a game. As I told you, I've seen the egg in action. Why do you think I'm not selling it? I'm giving up a lot of money, so I'd appreciate it if you'd stop acting like some idiot who doesn't understand what's going on."

"You have to understand that it's a lot worse than just the possibility of melting people." The Light Elf shook his head and looked down. "The energy in that egg can never be let out. It's more dark magic than anyone is used to or should be handling, and it could fuel all sorts of dangerous spells. If there were a way to destroy it, I would. The next best thing is to make sure no one gets their hands on it, which I can't do if you don't give it to me."

The tomb raider shrugged. "Unlike that cave in Argentina, no one knows where I keep my things. You can go ahead and try to track it down if you want to see the kind of precautions I've taken."

The human and the elf locked eyes, with the Professor looking on. No one spoke for a good thirty seconds before the Fixer looked away, sighed, and shook his head.

Correk stood. "You remind me of another stubborn woman I know." He shrugged. "If you ever change your mind, let me know. I will come and immediately take it off your hands and do my best to handle it."

Shay snorted. "That's just the thing. My hands will never touch it. Have a good night, Correk."

He shook his head. "After this conversation, I don't think I can."

7

Shay paced back and forth in her living room, frowning. It'd been a calm few days, so of course, something had to happen. She could kick herself for not anticipating it. It wasn't like the risk wasn't there before, but now that the threat was on its way to her home, her stomach knotted.

I have to get ready. What if they do something I'm not ready for?

She shook her head. "This is a disaster waiting to happen. A big disaster."

Alison smiled at her from the couch. "Seriously, Aunt Shay? You really think that? With all the stuff you deal with, it doesn't seem like this would be a big deal. It's just your friends coming to visit your place for the first time." She chuckled. "Some of Dad's OCD is wearing off on you."

The tomb raider stopped pacing and shook her head. "Look, I haven't exactly been forthcoming on all the details of my life with these women. They've been badgering me for a while about coming over, and I always found excuses, but I guess I was just too tired or something. The next thing I knew I had agreed to this little visit."

"But they're your friends. I know you told a few lies, but you like them, right?"

Shay sighed and nodded. "You have to understand that things work better when they're compartmentalized. That's how I've been living my life. It's why I've been able to have normal friends but still do tomb raiding and help James and all that."

"But you have Dad now, and it's not like you're in the same position you were before. If you're going to picnics with cops and guys from Camp Brownstone, things just aren't that separate. Besides, what could possibly go wrong with a few of your friends stopping by to check out your place?"

Shay shrugged. "I learned a long time ago that the answer to that question is almost always 'a lot.' For now, don't do any magic in front of them."

Alison sighed. "You think it would scare them?"

The tomb raider shook her head. "No. The opposite. I think they'll get excited and start acting like this is a magical theme park, and they'll want to see you do stunts. I wouldn't be half surprised if they don't recognize you from all the news coverage of the adoption hearing, but fortunately, they aren't the kind of women who pay a lot of attention to the news. It's one of the reasons I like hanging out with them. It's all light and breezy."

"I don't get it."

Shay shrugged. "Sometimes it's just nice to relax and

not have to worry about anything after having to worry about so much on a job."

"I can understand that." Alison smiled. "Then you should do just that—relax and not worry so much. It'll be fine. You're acting like this is a tomb raid, but it's just your friends stopping by."

Shay chuckled, some of the tension draining from her face. "When did you get so wise, Alison?"

"This year at school." The teen grinned.

"You're right, though. This isn't one of the warehouses, and my gear is hidden. If I can handle tomb raids, I can handle a few women coming over to my place who just want to chat and have a good time."

Or are those famous last words?

A light knock sounded from the door, and Shay walked over to open it. Kara, Bella, and Janelle stood on the other side. Kara held a long metal tube connected to a wide, enclosed base.

Okay, this is starting out a little weird.

Shay blinked. She had no clue what the item was, but she motioned them inside, and her friends rushed into the living room.

"Welcome." The tomb raider pointed to Alison. "This is Alison. She's my boyfriend's kid. She's home for the summer from boarding school. Alison, these are my friends Janelle, Kara, and Bella."

Alison offered them a bright smile. "It's nice to meet all of you."

Janelle tilted her head, a slight frown on her face. "I feel like I've seen you before. I was about to ask what high school you go to, but you go to boarding school?"

"Yes, in Virginia."

"Huh. Maybe it's déjà vu."

Alison shrugged. "Maybe I just have that kind of face. It's nice to meet you all." She rose to give them all gentle handshakes.

Bella winked at Shay. "Boarding school, huh? That can't be cheap. Nobody poor sends their kid to boarding school. Didn't know your new guy was rich, but you do seem to have a habit of landing rich boyfriends. Lucky you."

Shay let out a slight chuckle. She'd told them more than a few lies to cover for some of her expensive electronics and vehicles. She half-wondered if they thought she was some sort of academic gold digger.

Better that than an ex-killer.

Kara set her strange contraption in the middle of Shay's living room. Something sloshed inside it. "You should have had us over a long time ago." She ran her hand down the long tube. "And we should have used this sooner than later. I can already…sense the negative energy here."

"Negative energy? What are you talking about?" Shay frowned. "That's not some sort of weird bong, is it?"

Alison laughed. "Aunt Shay, how could you ask your friends that?"

She shrugged. "Just asking. I have no idea what the hell that thing is, and I don't want your dad yelling at me later."

The three women laughed.

Kara grinned. "It's not a bong. It's a smudge pot. I've already got sage in it. We need to do a smudge cleansing of the negative energy of your home."

Shay stared at the smudge pot. "Which consists of what, exactly?"

"We light the oil in the pot and burn the herbs. It'll make a lot of smoke, and the herbs will help clear out the negative energy. We'll take turns." She patted her purse. "Got some crystals in here to help spread the positive energy and absorb residual negative energy. Chanting and a little dancing will help, too."

Shay rubbed the back of her neck. "That thing looks pretty big. Can't we get something smaller or just burn some incense?"

Kara shook her head. "Nope, we need serious power for a serious cleanse. It's like getting the oil changed in your car, and since you don't even know about it, that means you've built up more negative energy than I can sense. You're lucky we got here when we did."

Shay shot a glance at Alison. The teen shrugged and smiled.

Yeah, if there were negative energy in my place, she'd be able to see it, but no reason to be a bitch about it to my friends. They are only trying to help in their own weird way.

The tomb raider eyed the smudge pot. "That makes sense. Negative energy, huh?"

"Prepared to be seriously wowed by the power of smudging. This is really ancient and powerful stuff. I'm kind of surprised you haven't heard of it before. I'm pretty sure the Oricerans invented it."

Shay shrugged. "I've heard of using herbs to spiritually cleanse an area, just not smudging."

The tomb raider managed not to burst out laughing. For all her concern with the truth and acceptance of the power of many magical rituals in light of Oriceran, some things still remained ridiculous, and since moving to California, she'd found she ran into the ridiculous at a higher rate than she had in New York. If all it took was a little incense and a few crystals to remove negative energy, the magical world would have been a much different place, and people like James wouldn't even have a job.

Plus, it was hard to even think the word "smudging" without being amused.

Couldn't they have at least given it a different name?

Shay grimaced at a sudden realization. "I'm gonna have to turn off my smoke alarms, though. Don't want the fire department showing up to ruin my house cleanse and add more negative energy."

"Good plan," Janelle commented.

I can't believe I'm agreeing to let them fill my house with smoke. Sometimes friendship's a real pain in the ass. Or smoke in the face.

Kara furrowed her brow. "It does create a lot of smoke, but it's for the best. Can't let that negative energy build up. If you do, it can attract evil spirits, and with all that magic flowing around, that's more of a threat than ever. My cousin didn't smudge enough, and they ended up with an honest-to-goodness ghost, I swear."

The tomb raider's few encounters with ghosts had been more annoying than frightening, but she wasn't about to let her friends know about that. She also doubted that Kara's cousin's ghost had anything to do with not smudging enough.

Shay gave Kara a solemn nod, trying her best not to laugh. "Yeah, I'm sure ghosts hate smudging. Scared little white-sheet assholes."

The faint smirk on Alison's face told Shay she was

enjoying this as much as the tomb raider. The girl, after all, was half-Drow and even her basic sensory experience was centered around magic. Her school days were dripping with actual enchantment and wonder, not just West Coast wannabes waving crystals.

Shay cleared her throat. "Before we start chasing out any negative energy, let me give you a quick tour of the place. We can open the windows as we do it. Two birds. One stone."

The women all nodded, eager smiles on their faces.

Fifteen minutes later, they finished a thorough tour of all the rooms on both stories of the converted brownstone. They praised Shay's interior decorating skills as they reiterated the dangerous build-up of negative energy that must have occurred during her time living there. Kara stressed that a poltergeist might manifest soon if they didn't smudge.

"Especially since you're an archaeologist," Kara commented as they came back into the living room.

Shay blinked. "Huh? What does being an archaeologist have to do with negative energy?"

"I know it's for science and all, but you're always digging up old bones and stuff. There have to be a few ghosts around. They won't always get why you're doing it."

Not as many ghosts as you might think, but you're more right than not. Wonder what they would say if I told them I faced off against a demonic chicken?

They would probably find that harder to believe than the

ghosts. Shit, I was there, *and I still barely believe it. I think I'd rather deal with more ghosts than evil poultry or weird-ass frogmen.*

The tomb raider almost snorted. Her friends might not know what she did for a living, but they'd gotten closer to the truth with some of her problems than she would have ever expected.

Kara marched over to the smudge pot. "It's time to get our smudge on."

Alison grinned. "This ought to be good."

Kara looked at the girl. "Have you ever participated in something like this?"

The teen glanced at Shay then back at her friend. "Not this, but at my boarding school they worry about negative energy. We have to do stuff to get rid of it."

Shay's friends nodded.

"That's very enlightened of them," Kara offered.

I don't even want to know what sort of magical cleaning they make them do in the dorms at that school.

Kara marched over to the smudge pot and tugged on a small oil-soaked wick to pull it out farther. She produced a lighter from her pocket and lit the wick, scurrying away a little too fast for Shay's taste.

I wonder if my insurance covers fires started by smudge pots.

A healthy flame emerged from the top, and thick aromatic smoke poured from the pot.

Shay shook her head. This seemed more like something a SWAT team did to holed-up criminals than something a person would do on purpose to help their house.

Kara stood near the smudge pot and extended her

hand, a large blue crystal in her palm. She half-closed her eyes.

The tomb raider made her way over to the couch to whisper to Alison.

"Is that crystal actually magic?"

Alison shook her head. "Nothing they're doing is magical at all," the girl whispered back. "But watching their soul energy is too much fun. They believe it all, and they're genuinely excited to help you."

"Guess they aren't really hurting anything…I hope."

Shay stood and blinked her eyes a few times, the smoke already quite thick. Kara danced around the smudging pot, chanting while shaking her crystal.

I can't believe I agreed to this. I guess it's the thought that counts.

James' F-350 screeched to a halt in Shay's driveway. Thick smoke poured out of the windows and doors. His heart rate sped up.

"Fuck," the bounty hunter rumbled. He scanned the place, looking for a collapsed wall or any sign of a rocket attack.

He threw open the door of his truck and hopped out, his hand drifting inside his jacket. A brief thought of bonding with his amulet crossed his mind, but he didn't want to use it if it were a minor threat.

Instead, James yanked out something easier to understand and far less vocal about its work: his .45.

Maybe it has nothing to do with criminals. Maybe a gas line exploded. Shit.

He jogged over to the open door, raising his gun. If anything had happened to Alison or Shay, his destruction of the Harriken would look like a minor inconvenience compared to what he would do. Even if it weren't criminals, he'd go after every contractor if it was the result of shoddy workmanship.

James burst through the front door, half-expecting mercenaries, or perhaps a witch or a few cartel members. He didn't expect Shay's three friends to be dancing, laughing, and chanting around something in the center of her living room.

What...the...hell?

Alison watched them from the couch a huge grin on her face. Shay leaned against a wall, more restrained amusement on her features.

Why the fuck do they have a smudge pot inside? I thought you used those outside in orchards. I'll never understand women.

The bounty hunter blinked and shoved his gun back into its holster before the women noticed.

James started to back out of the door when Janelle spotted him.

She gasped and pointed. "That's why I recognize Alison. From the news. From the hearing when they tried to block her adoption."

The bounty hunter grunted and looked at his recently adopted daughter. She gave him a thin little grin and a shrug.

"You're James Brownstone," Janelle all but shrieked. "And she's Alison Brownstone."

The two other women stopped and stared at him before pivoting as a group toward Shay.

"You didn't tell us you were dating James Brownstone," they shouted in unison. "*The* James Brownstone!"

James groaned and scrubbed a hand over his face.

Shay shrugged. "Surprise."

8

Shay smirked when James' hand twitched. He picked up his pizza with a frown and took a bite. It'd been hard enough to get him to agree to the date, so she wasn't surprised to see him less than relaxed.

The man can kill hundreds of gangsters without blinking, but push him outside his comfort zone for a few hours and he's like some nervous little kid. KISS screwed you over, James. You should have lived by AETU, Always Expect The Unexpected.

Shay sighed. "She'll be fine alone at my place. She's not a little kid, James. If she can take the train from Virginia to LA by herself, I think she can last a few hours at home without Dad. She was walking the streets by herself before you even met her if you remember."

"Doesn't mean I can't worry." James grunted. "Just so you know, Alison says it still smells funny from your friend's weird shit yesterday."

The tomb raider chuckled. "It does. I think it's gonna take a while to get the smell out, but at least I don't have any negative energy in my house." She laughed and picked up her water to take a sip.

He snorted. "Negative energy. Magic's real now, so why do people still believe in bullshit?"

"Knowing magic's real means there's a greater than zero chance that any bit of bullshit is true." Shay shrugged.

James shook his head. "Your friends are strange."

"Most of *your* friends are ex-gang members or criminal information brokers. Not exactly a normal group of guys." She snickered.

He frowned. "Information brokers? You talking about Tyler? He's not my friend. He's just a guy I know." He pointed at her. "And don't call him a frenemy. I fucking hate that word."

Shay rolled her eyes. "Yeah, he's totally not your friend. You guys just hatch idiot plans together to make money all the time, and he constantly bets on you kicking ass. Hell, after the hearing, he pretty much said he was your friend. Was half-weepy about it, even."

"It's weird to think of Tyler as my friend." James shook his head. "At least he's not coming over to my house and trying to set it on fire, unlike *your* friends."

"Yet. I'm sure if he can find a way to make money betting on Brownstone arson, he will."

James grunted. "Wouldn't put it past him. The guy's not a total piece of shit, but he's still a slippery little snake."

"Enough about your weird friends for now." Shay set her glass down and folded her hands in front of her. "So, last week, when you agreed to go out on this date with me, do you remember what else you said?"

"I have a photographic memory. Of course, I remember." He shrugged.

"And what did you agree to after dinner?"

James' face paled, and he winced. "Shit. That I'd go wherever you wanted afterward." He rubbed his neck. "I just figured you meant a movie or something. Why? You got some weird shit planned?"

Shay enjoyed the slight panic in her man's eyes. Seeing the mighty James Brownstone, Scourge of Harriken and the Granite Ghost, worried about what she might have in store made her want to throw her head back and cackle.

I should take a picture of him.

"You don't have to look like I'm gonna drop you into a nest of Drow and despair bugs. It's not some big, twisted plan. I just want to go dancing. Normal, everyday dancing, like normal people who aren't bounty hunters and tomb raiders do."

James grunted. "Dancing? I don't dance." He shrugged. "I kick ass, and I barbeque."

"It's called flexibility, James." Shay shook a finger at him. "And it doesn't matter. You at least have to go to a club with me, because you promised to go wherever I wanted, and I want to go to a club."

He shrugged. "Fine. That doesn't mean I'm dancing."

"Don't be so afraid. Dancing's just like sex, except with your clothes on." She smirked.

James grunted.

The pounding base thrummed through Shay's body in time with the changing of the kaleidoscopic lights overhead. The thick scents of men's cologne, women's perfume, and everybody's sweat mingled in the air, not letting anyone forget even for a second where they were.

James stood against the wall, his arms hanging at his side and tension radiating out of every pore as he frowned at the thick crowd filling the dance floor. It was like he expected a group of magical assassins to bust through the wall and go after him at any second.

Shay tried not to laugh at her poor uncomfortable boyfriend. It might take years to whip him into shape.

Can't be too surprised. For a guy who likes simple and straight-forward, a crowded club must feel like a slap in the face. He needs to loosen up a little, though, and, shit, I want to go dancing sometimes with someone other than the girls. Is it so wrong to go dancing with your man?

She needed to give him a reason to care, and a reason to understand the power that came with dancing.

Shay sashayed over to him, wrapping her arms around his neck and putting her face right next to his.

"You look like you're trying to pass a kidney stone." She snickered. "Try to relax a little. You could have a fun time if you let yourself."

"This place is fucking loud," he rumbled. "An assassin could go to town in here, and people wouldn't realize for an hour that someone's been killed."

"It's a club. It's supposed to be loud, and most people aren't worried about assassins. They aren't exactly James Brownstone." Shay laughed. "Or even me. It's just a club where people go to drink and dance. You know, have fun."

James frowned. "How are people supposed to chat when it's so fucking loud?"

Shay laughed. "They aren't. Their bodies are supposed to do the talking for them. Come on, let's do a little dance-talking."

She shimmied backward a little, letting her arms drop and trace down the thick, powerful muscles in his arms until she reached his hands and tugged lightly.

James shook his head. Despite the noise, she could still make out what he had to say.

"I agreed to go wherever you wanted. I didn't agree to *do* whatever you wanted."

A blond pretty boy sauntered up to Shay and shouted to be heard. "I see that guy doesn't want to dance. I'd be more than happy to dance with a beautiful woman like you. That guy doesn't appreciate what he's got."

Shay was surprised the pretty boy didn't recognize James, especially given how much he'd been on television in recent weeks. She didn't say anything back, instead waiting to see how her anti-dancing boyfriend would react.

The bounty hunter stomped over toward the man and let a loud growl. "Get the fuck out of here, asshole, or I'll punt you through a fucking wall."

The pretty boy's eyes widened, and he ran off, dodging through the crowd like he expected James to open fire on him at any second.

Shay cackled. "Are you kidding me right now? I thought *I* used to overreact to annoying guys in clubs, but you make me look like the Queen of Restraint."

He shrugged. "Fine, I'll dance a little if it'll make you

happy." He muttered as he stepped forward. "This shit's gonna be worse than the Bard of Filth Competition. Dancing. Yeah. Whatever."

Shay placed her hands on his body as she started moving in time with the music. The poor man tried, but either he had a supernaturally bad sense of rhythm or the tension still suffusing him wouldn't let him shake it.

The sad truth was that James Brownstone had zero groove. Hell, he had negative groove.

The tomb raider grinned, turning around to grind her ass against him for a bit. James grunted, and she let out another merry laugh.

I don't even care if he is dancing. I've got James Brownstone on a dance floor in a club. That's a victory in itself. Too bad I'm not taking video of this.

The tension stopped radiating off James the minute they stepped into his F-350. He let out a sigh of relief as if he'd just escaped a hostile den of Oriceran assassins.

Shay reached over to pat him on the arm. "I know that probably made you almost have a stroke, but I like that you at least tried. Sometimes you just got to push life, you know?"

He turned the key, and his engine roared to life. "Next time, I think I would prefer to be dropped into a bunch of angry Drow or back in that freaky-ass lab in Las Vegas."

The tomb raider gave him a seductive smile. "Good boys who do what they're told get rewards later."

James grinned. "I did what I was told."

They pulled out of the parking lot. A few minutes of silence passed, with Shay smiling out the window.

Nice. The last couple of days have been nice. I needed something to clean out the old thoughts after that shit in Argentina.

Just pizza and dancing, nothing special on the surface, but it was hard to ignore how the last few days had been something unusual. Spending time with Alison felt like the most natural thing in the world, and now it wasn't a big deal to have an open relationship with James. It got inconvenient when people recognized him, but they mostly wanted his autograph or to buy him barbeque. Not much she could do about dating one of the most famous bounty hunters in the country.

Part of her worried about someone recognizing her and deciding it was a good time to take her out, but they would have to contend with James as well as her. Neither of them went anywhere without guns. Shay was almost always carrying at least one adamantine knife, and her man almost always had his amulet on him, even if it wasn't bonded. Unless an attacker killed them instantly, they were in for a world of pain.

"We should stop somewhere," James rumbled, breaking the silence.

"Stop somewhere? You hungry again? Yeah, I know you're the man who'd eat a whole cow if they'd offered it to you, but you had so much pizza earlier. I'm honestly surprised."

He shook his head. "Not that kind of thing. You know, more like dessert shit. Ice cream. Hot summer night and all that."

Shay smiled, but then it faded. She couldn't push the

image of a melting ice cream cone out of her mind, the thick, dripping liquid all too strong a reminder of the poor bastard in Argentina.

Too fucking soon.

She shrugged. "Screw ice cream. How about we go home and have some hot and sweaty fun?"

James grinned. "Not gonna complain about that."

9

───────

Shay stifled a yawn the next morning as she sat in front of the office computer in Warehouse Two. James' stamina was as superhuman as everything else about him, which always made spending a night with him a careful balance of judging pleasure in the moment versus soreness in the future. She wasn't always sure she always picked the right side of that equation, but she never felt bad about it either.

Not like I'm running off on a tomb raid today. It'll be okay.

She tapped away at the computer, snickering and pushing the thoughts of her alien lover out of her head. Peyton wasn't there, and she couldn't help but wonder where her assistant was.

His earlier issues with getting to Warehouse Two in a timely manner had gone away, and she hadn't had to worry much about busting his balls about showing up. She'd settled into a comfortable rhythm of just expecting him to be there when she showed up.

"I'll give him a few more minutes before I call him."

Shay took a deep breath. It'd been a while since she last hit the dark web for a deep dive into the forums and sites catering to people employed in her original profession of the not-so-kindly art of paid murder. Given how she'd let more than a few people, including James' friends, meet her, it wouldn't be a bad idea to double-check and make sure no one new was coming after her.

I wonder how long I can keep this up. Fake professor by day, tomb raider by night. Won't have to make any big decisions unless the school wants me to do more than guest lecture. What do I do if they ask?

She clicked around with her mouse as she cruised along to the kinds of websites that kept the NSA and FBI up at night. Improvements in cryptography in recent decades had done a lot to facilitate personal privacy, while at the same time allowing criminals to be even bolder on the net.

So many people out there want so many other people dead. Shit. If they just had the balls, they could do it themselves and cut out the middleman. Why not save the money? Fucking pussies. I'm annoyed I helped so many of them.

Shay snorted and shook her head. She started scrolling down a forum message board and stopped. Her heart kicked up as she read a message and spotted a familiar picture.

"Son of a bitch. You've got to be kidding me. You fucking moron." The tomb raider pinched the bridge of her nose. "Talk about no good deed going unpunished!"

The message was a request for a hit but had raised an unusual amount of discussion because of its nature. Hitmen and professional killers tended to prefer straight-forward fixed payments, but this hit promised a fifty-percent cut of an inherited fortune once the hitman could find the target, kill the target, and drop off the body in front of a police station of all things to facilitate rapid confirmation of the death of the target.

Shay shook head. "Talk about balls, you arrogant asshole."

The elaborate requirements might not make sense to the average hitman, but the picture of the target in the forum made it very clear both why so much money was being offered and the reasoning behind the request.

The target was Peyton.

Shay shook her head. Their efforts had taken Randy's access to serious money away. They'd tried to Scrooge him into behaving, and the financial assault was supposed to eliminate the need to put some bullets into the man, but now he was trying the next step—hiring thugs to go kill a man who was supposed to be already dead by offering ridiculous amounts of future money.

That Peyton's brother had done that was irritating enough, but the fact that a group of killers had agreed to the damned deal ruined Shay's morning.

You dumbasses. Why would you take a hit with a contingency-based payment plan? That's just bad business. Unfortunately for you, I'm gonna prove to you why it's such bad business.

"Fucking Randy." She shook her head. "You're dumber than the Harriken. You should have given up when you had the chance since I'm fucking through with looking the other way with you."

Shay took a few breaths and picked up her phone. Peyton needed and deserved to know what was going on.

She gritted her teeth. Or was she already too late? He wasn't at the warehouse even though she'd expected him. There was one possible fatal reason that might be the case.

She dialed his number. One ring. Two rings.

"Hello," he answered on the third ring.

The relief that washed through Shay surprised her. "Where the fuck are you, Peyton?"

"My place still. Sorry, I overslept."

"Who is that, Peyton?" called a female voice in the background.

"Just my boss."

Shay hadn't met the woman, but she'd already done enough surveillance on her to recognize the voice. Amber, Peyton's girlfriend.

The tomb raider sighed. No reason to ruin both their mornings.

"What's up?" he asked. "Or are you just pissed that I'm not there?"

"Don't worry about it, Peyton. Not like I'm aching to go on another job right away. Take your time. I've got my own shit to look into anyway."

"You sure?" The doubt in his voice almost made Shay laugh.

"Yeah, I'm sure."

"Everything okay? This just doesn't sound like you. Do we need some sort of distress codes for phone calls so I can know you're okay?"

Shay snorted. "Even *I* can't be a bitch 24/7."

"I don't know about that."

"Handle your girlfriend," Shay snapped, "and I'll handle shit here."

Peyton sighed. "Okay. If you need me, just let me know."

"Let's just say I'm sure I don't need you for what I'm about to do."

James shook his head as he stepped out of the black van with a ski mask on. "Why didn't you just fucking kill this guy a while ago? You chewed me out about not killing Lars Hansen's buddies, but you've let this fucker slide when he already tried to have Peyton killed?"

Shay sighed and slipped on her ski mask. The bounty hunter did have a point. It wasn't so much that she gave that much of a shit about being hypocritical. It was more that she found it annoying to have to explain it.

"Because Peyton didn't want me to, and it's his brother, so I figured he got to make the call."

The bounty hunter shook his head. "Just saying, even now it'd be easier to just go directly to him and kill him if he's your big problem instead of all this complicated shit you've set up."

The tomb raider shook her head. "Peyton's not me, and I don't think he could handle it if I pulled the trigger. It doesn't matter that his brother's been trying to kill him for a while now or that we've given the asshole every chance in the world to walk away." She shrugged. "What can I say? He's fucking soft, okay?"

Shay patted her tactical harness to confirm she had extra magazines and grenades. If everything went according to plan she might not have to kill anyone, but with a dozen men on the way, they needed to be prepared in case shit went south.

She looked at James. "You got Whispy Doom on?"

James shook his head and slapped his chest. "Not bonded. Don't need the amulet for only twelve normal guys. I feel like he's got more of an attitude now. I think I liked it better when I couldn't understand what the fuck he was saying."

Shay shrugged. "If you end up getting killed, I'm gonna mock you at your funeral."

He grunted. "I'll keep that in mind."

They threw open a side door to the old abandoned factory where they'd hidden the van just inside the loading bay. The pair hurried outside to get into position on both sides of their kill zone.

There were a lot of moving parts in the plan where things could go wrong. Shay had to cover up the contract on Peyton's life before he found out about it while simultaneously leaving breadcrumbs for the hit team. It'd taken several days of time and effort, especially since she'd had to do it under Peyton's nose. The big risk was actually giving the team the information that their target might be in LA.

She'd anonymously reached out to Tyler and a few other information brokers across town to provide them a juicy little tidbit: a hit team was setting a trap for the Peyton kill team, with the relevant people meeting in an abandoned industrial park.

In minutes, the future of Peyton and Randy Coolidge would be determined.

Two vans and an Audi with tinted windows were parked outside the closest factory, all with dummies inside.

Jammers choked the EM waves in the area, stopping drones from getting a closer look or launching any aerial assaults.

James and Shay already knew the men were en route. She had been tracking them by drone before she activated the jammers.

If anything, the jamming would make the hitmen more apt to believe a meeting of killers was occurring. No one jammed an area unless they were trying to hide something.

Anyone who wanted to finish off the alleged ambush team would need to get up close and personal.

Shay pulled her magical silencer out of a pouch in her harness and screwed it onto her 9mm. James would make the big noise, but she'd break her typical pattern and be a little less up close and personal with her kills.

It'd have to be a careful balance. An ambush where you wanted to kill everyone was easy enough to pull off, but one where you were trying to leave some survivors and pass along a message without being obvious? Not so much.

James jogged toward several rusted oil drums and crouched behind them. Shay scrambled up a rickety ladder until she hit the partially collapsed roof of a nearby building.

Hope they don't have real-time satellite coverage. If they do, this will be over really quickly.

Shay snorted. This wasn't a CIA wetwork squad, just some run-of-the-mill killers. She and James had decapitated an entire cartel and the Harriken. These guys were roaches in comparison.

The rumble of engines sounded, and she crouched.

Three black SUVs shot down a side street, screeching as they took a hard turn into the industrial park.

The tomb raider grinned. She almost felt sorry for the bastards. Almost.

One of the SUVs sped past the bait vehicles Shay and James had set up and turned hard to block them in. The other two stopped behind them. Rifles poked from open windows and opened fire.

The guns spat bullet after bullet, their loud reports overlapping and echoing in the lonely industrial park. Glass shattered on the bait cars, and the dummies jerked with each bullet striking them. Fake blood from the dummies splattered all over the glass.

I knew it was worth it to add the extra touch. It's the small details that really sell something like this.

Shay smirked at the mock massacre going on beneath her. A brief halt in the hail of bullets ended seconds later as all the hitmen reloaded and opened fire again. Finally, after a long couple of minutes, the assault ceased.

Dozens of bullet holes punctured the bait cars. Red splotches lay in the street and the shattered windows. Almost all the tires were now flat.

A cautious hitman in a suit stepped out of the lead SUV, automatic rifle in hand, and crept toward the Audi with his gun up. A few others exited the other vehicles and made their way toward the vans.

Almost there, asshole. Almost there. Just keep going.

Shay reached down to her belt and pulled out three EMP grenades. She trusted her throwing arm, but with three vehicles it didn't matter. She really only needed to ensure two were taken out.

"What the fuck?" the first hitman shouted. "There ain't anyone in here. It's just dummies."

"You fucking sure? Maybe we just jacked them up so much they looked like dummies now."

Shay rolled her eyes. It was an important reminder that not every professional killer was an intelligent woman with an interest in ancient history and a penchant for wanting to uncover the truth.

With three quick tosses, she sent the EMP grenades flying toward the SUVs.

"What the fuck is that?" the first hitman shouted.

A loud buzz and crackle filled the air, and the SUVs all died.

"Randy Coolidge sends his regards, assholes," Shay shouted, her voice echoing among the cluster of buildings and difficult to trace. "You call that an ambush? We'll show you a fucking ambush, you pieces of shit. This is what you get for being so greedy. Should have only asked for ten percent."

James threw a couple of frag grenades from behind the oil drums right after her speech. Shay raised her 9mm and put two rounds into the first hitman. He dropped to the ground with a scream.

The frag grenades exploded near the other men. Their echoing cries of pain further added to the confusion.

Shay started unloading her pistol into the two black SUVs, while James blasted away with his .45, bullet after bullet striking the vehicles. This time the shattering glass and blood splatters were all too real markers of actual men dying.

James took the opportunity to toss another couple of grenades while Shay reloaded.

They'd concentrated their fire on the back two SUVs and the men outside. The doors to the front SUV opened and three men rushed out, sprinting away from the carnage.

Shay waited a few seconds and then put three rounds into the back of one of the men. That left two men fleeing.

She smiled. They'd killed enough to make their point. The tomb raider sent a couple of smoke grenades down at the ground. She doubted the men would realize the SUVs weren't burning in their confusion.

The tomb raider reloaded and slid down the ladder on the side of the building. She crouched against the wall, then spun around the corner, approaching the lead SUV while James came in from the other direction. Blood and bodies covered the ground.

A man groaned and crawled toward his weapon. Shay kicked it out of his grasp but didn't finish him off. She had a mask on, and his survival, in addition to the other two's, would only work better for the plan.

She strode toward the other two vehicles. Most of the men were dead, but a few had managed to survive.

Maybe a little overkill, but enough.

The tomb raider nodded to James and jogged toward the abandoned factory. He caught up with her as she pulled open the loading door.

"Still think it'd've been easier to just go kill Randy," James rumbled. "When the Harriken fucked with me, I went and killed the Harriken. I didn't trick the Nuevo Gulf Cartel into killing them."

"If only we could all be as honest with our feelings as you." Shay grinned and shook her head. "Nope. This way *they* waste him, and Peyton doesn't end up beating himself up over his piece-of-shit brother." She glanced over her shoulder. "Nicely done. A good mixture of brawn and brains. Won't be long now till Randy is no longer a problem."

10

A few days later, Shay sat on a bench in front of a fountain in the middle of the mall, scanning the crowd. A small bag from a jewelry shop sat in her lap, but she was focused instead on the arrival of one teenage girl with white-tipped black hair.

This is the ultimate test. You have all the people around here, but you can use the magolocation to help you navigate. Let's see if you can actually find me, Alison.

Shay chuckled. Finding a particular teenage girl with unusual hair in a mall was an exercise in false positives, not helped by the tomb raider disliking the fact that her back wasn't against a wall. The more she thought about it, the more she realized the only worse place to die than her kitchen would be the mall.

If she hadn't been concentrating, she might have missed the faint purple pulse. They still needed to figure out a way to perform the magolocation without it being visible, but in a crowded and raucous place like the mall, no one noticed anyway.

The tomb raider continued scanning the thronging humanity. She could never get over how so much had changed but also so little had changed at the same time. Despite the powerful magic now pouring into the world, the only difference someone might see at the mall was the occasional non-human customer, like a trio of elven women strolling out of an aromatherapy shop across the way.

Is this what culture does? Just keeps flowing in the rut it's in? We get magic back, and mostly we get criminals and terrorists with magic or an elf who cooks barbeque. Don't know if that's comforting or scary.

White hair emerged from the crowd. Alison glided between the crowds to the bench. She sat beside Shay, a triumphant smile on her face.

Shay nodded, giving the girl an answering smile. "All the way from the car to this fountain, and much better time than without the pulses. Still have some tweaking to do."

"Did you see the pulse I did just before I sat down?"

"Yeah. Like I said, some tweaking."

"It'll take a while to get used to, but I still think it's useful." Alison shrugged. "Not going to complain if you can get me the artifact to help me see more, though, and I'll keep trying to figure out a way to do it without it being so obvious."

Shay smiled. "Sounds like a good plan, and I'll definitely get that artifact for you. I'd like to give you a particular date, but my gnome friend isn't the kind of guy who responds well to deadlines."

Alison sighed. "Don't get me wrong. All this training

you and Dad have given me means a lot, and if I went back to school today, I'd go back feeling more confident." The teen smiled softly. "I know I bitched in the beginning, but I really do get it now."

Shay nodded. "Good. That's what practice and training do; they give you confidence. Did you see what I had in my lap with your last pulse?"

"Some sort of bag."

The tomb raider lifted the bag and held it out. Alison grabbed it with no hesitation. Even without the pulse, it seemed like her ability to judge item distances based on life energy from limbs had improved in recent weeks.

"What's in here?" Alison asked. "Even with the pulse, it's hard for me to tell. Small boxes. I'm assuming something inside them."

"Diamond earrings. Studs," Shay explained.

"That's nice, Aunt Shay, but I don't worry about jewelry much." Alison laughed. "Even with the pulse, it's not like I can see it. I do appreciate the thought though."

"I know. Just wanted to get you something nice. James gave you that pendant, which is pretty and functional, so I can at least give you something nice to remind you of me when you're at school. I don't know how long it'll take to get the artifact ready." Shay rubbed the back of her neck. "If I'd been thinking ahead, I would have scored you some lesser artifact jewelry."

"It's not a competition, Aunt Shay. I love you both." The girl fingered the chain of the Aegis Pendant. "And you don't have to give me things for me to think about you at school."

Shay looked away, her face burning. The girl's comment

struck her heart more than she'd expected. "Well, you can always just loan the earrings to a roommate then. Everyone likes a generous roommate."

Alison laughed. "Maybe I'll do that." Her smile faded a second later. "I just…don't get one thing, Aunt Shay. I didn't want to bring it up, but I guess now is as good a time as any."

"What's that?"

The girl looked down and frowned. "Not saying no one should have secrets, and I know a lot of the stuff with your job you try to keep quiet to keep things safer, but I still…" She sighed again.

Shay frowned. "What? Are you worried about me being a tomb raider? Not to brag, but I'm pretty damned good at my job. I know what I'm doing at this point, and now I typically even have Peyton supporting me. It's not like when I first started."

"It's not that."

"What is it, then?"

Alison shook her head. "I don't get why you've been hiding Lily from Dad and me."

The tomb raider sucked in a breath. Trying to deny the existence of the other girl was pointless since she was sitting in front of a half-Drow lie detector. Shay took a long, deep breath. "How did you know?"

"Peyton told me."

Shay frowned.

That son of a bitch. It wasn't his secret to share.

Alison shook her head. "I can see the anger in your energy, Aunt Shay, but he told me to tell you that it's not a state secret, so don't threaten him with firearms." She smiled as she said it. "And I think he was right to tell me."

Shay took a few deep, cleansing breaths. Peyton did have a point. Alison and James knew about multiple warehouses and her tomb raiding career. Both knew how to keep secrets, and Lily's existence paled in comparison to things like James controlling a wish on Alison's behalf or James knowing Shay used to be a vicious professional killer.

The tomb raider scrubbed a hand down her face and blew out a breath. "It's not like I never planned to tell you or him. It was just hard to figure out how to do it. Like I told you the other day, the way I've handled all this stuff is by compartmentalizing my life. Everyone has their little boxes. I thought that would make it easier, not just for me but for everyone else, but lately, I've realized that wasn't the best plan."

A brief look of sadness passed over Alison's face. "I'm not saying it's wrong to have secrets. I've got a few myself."

Shay shrugged. "Not even gonna ask. I know if you need help you'll ask for it."

The girl nodded. "I...do kind of want to meet her, though. Lily. I mean, we're similar. Orphans. Half-elves. The same kickass woman has taken an interest in training us."

Shay chuckled. "She's pretty secretive. Meeting her isn't all that easy. Even with me, most of it is on her schedule, and she only shows up when she wants to. I can try to call her, but I can't always reach her."

"I get that. Just saying."

"We also had a nasty experience on our last raid. She might not want to show up for a while, and I can't blame her."

Alison nodded. "You think she'll avoid you the rest of the summer?"

Shay shook her head. "I honestly don't know, but if the chance comes up for you to meet her, I'll see what I can do."

"That's all I ask." The teen kicked her legs, a wistful look on her face.

Why did Peyton suddenly tell her about Lily? And why does she care that much? I hope she's not jealous. Wait...

Shay furrowed her brow. "Do you miss your friends at school?"

Alison blinked and looked up. "What?"

"We've got you hanging out with bounty hunters, cops, and tomb raiders, but not anybody your age. I was just wondering if you missed your friends."

"Yeah, I do." Alison shrugged. "But I love being home with you and Dad. I want to spend more time with you, and as for Lily, some of it's about her and some it's just about..." She sighed. "It's going to seem silly."

"I'm dating your dad. He's Captain Silly sometimes between his KISS and the barbeque obsession. I still can't get over that ridiculous pit he and Sergeant Mack had built."

Alison laughed and shrugged. "I just want to know more about you, Aunt Shay. Even the parts you aren't proud of, but I'm willing to wait until you're ready." She pointed to her face. "You forget, I can see your soul. I know how beautiful it is, even if you doubt it."

Shay blinked and stared at the girl.

If you say so, Alison.

11

Shay slipped on her gloves and began stretching along with Aaron, Lana, and the other members of Free-to-Move. They'd already taken a helpful elevator to the top of an eight-story office building downtown. The streetlights had flicked on with the setting sun, and the bright lights of the city pushed away much of the darkness but left more than a few pockets in shadow.

She smiled. Alison wanted to do parkour. If they could improve her little pulse technique, or if Tubal-Cain could come up with something practical, it might be less of a dream and more of a reality.

Hell, if she really gets good with her pulse technique, she might be better at night than I am.

Lana grinned at Shay. "You're in a good mood."

"I'm always in a good mood."

The other woman laughed. "If you say so."

"Just thinking about friends and family, is all."

Lana's face scrunched. "I always think of them more

around holidays." She shrugged. "When they aren't bothering me online."

Shay moved to the edge of the roof to stare down at the flow of traffic up and down the road. "Family's kind of a new thing for me, to be honest."

She chuckled about feeling so talkative, let alone on this particular subject and with a parkour-club acquaintance. The lack of any substantial link to any other part of her life was part of the motivation. The walls that had allowed compartmentalization had begun to fall one by one, but at least the parkour group was still far more interested in her skills than her background.

She'd managed to avoid ending up on any news footage outside of the media circus that was Alison's adoption hearing, but the more time she spent in public around James, the more chance that eventually everyone would start recognizing her, if only as James Brownstone's girlfriend.

Do I even have to worry about anyone else anymore? The cartel's gone. Yulia might have fucked with my raids, but she keeps a pretty low profile, and I doubt she's gonna come here just to try to kill me.

Lana laughed, snapping Shay out of her thoughts. "How can family be new to you?"

Shay shrugged. "I left home pretty young. Spent a long time depending only on myself. Caring about other people —that's what's new."

"I can understand that. You had to make your own way, but now you've changed, and it's weird to look back at even who you were.'

"Yeah, changed a lot." Shay let out a wistful sigh. "Still

trying to wrap my head around a lot of it." She shook out her head. Brooding was for James. "A fun night tour of the city, huh?"

Lana nodded. "Yep. We might even run into the Night Spiders."

Shay looked away to hide her smile. She'd seen Lily and the magical teens in action and could testify to the impressiveness of their enhanced parkour moves, but being a little open about her background didn't mean she was ready to start telling every random person all her secrets.

"Oh? You interested in them?" the tomb raider asked.

Lana chuckled. "Just, ever since you asked about next-level parkour a while back, I've been thinking about them a lot more." She shrugged. "Maybe at this point, I want just to know the truth of whether they exist. The only person I've seen who could pull off the kind of stuff they do is Marcus, and the idea of a bunch of people like him blows my mind."

"We could get lucky and see them."

Shay was half-tempted to text Lily to ask for a little display. Her smile faded, and the thought drifted away. Lily probably wouldn't want to be around her for a while.

That's what it means to be a tomb raider, kid. Impressive magic, and senseless violence and death.

Aaron waved his arms. "Is everyone ready? Remember that we changed tonight's final rendezvous to that frozen yogurt place. If you're not going to stop by, text me, so we know you didn't die."

Everyone laughed. Shay didn't. Bouncing around the city at night at high speed was dangerous. She could never understand why no one else seemed to think that.

Aaron and Lana ran toward the edge of the building. Shay ran after them.

Tonight's the night. I keep coming in third or fourth, but I'm gonna go all-out.

The tomb raider sprinted full speed toward the edge of the building and leaped, soaring into the night sky. A stream of yellow and red lights streamed beneath her. LA night traffic.

The flight lasted only for a few seconds before she landed on the next roof with a smooth roll that brought her back to her feet with almost no loss of momentum. Lana appeared at her side and rushed past her.

Oh, the chase is on, huh?

Shay grinned. She picked up the pace, sprinting after the woman. The thud of Aaron's footfalls sounded right behind her.

Lana jumped over the side of the building, but Shay's heart didn't speed up. She'd studied the course as thoroughly as she might the background for a tomb raid. No surprises tonight, just a chance to prove her skills.

The tomb raider followed the other woman over the edge. Lana had landed on metal stairs and was already halfway down them. Shay jumped over a handrail and fell toward the bottom. She caught another rail about six feet above the street while the other woman hopped back and forth using a less dramatic strategy.

Shay hit the street and ran toward a nearby alley, now in the lead. She didn't sprint through the alley. They still had many miles to go on the course, and exhausting herself in the few first minutes wouldn't help her prove her skills.

I need to win tonight. I need to show them my determination.

A jog brought her out of the alley and toward a fence. Lana and Aaron were a few yards behind her on either side. She spotted a USPS mailbox and ran toward it. With a clean vault off the box, she cleared the fence. Lana and Aaron both hit the fence directly and scrambled over it.

A grin broke out on the tomb raider's face as she ran from the fence toward the darkened multi-level parking garage. Another quick vault over a gate sent her inside, the other two close behind, and the rest of the club much farther back.

The runners followed the spiraling concrete structure up for two stories before Shay broke toward an open space between a large truck and an obnoxiously yellow Porsche.

Someone's overcompensating.

Shay jumped onto the railing and pushed off without a second of hesitation. She'd long since learned that was the difference between her and the others like Lana or Aaron, or even Lily and her friends. Some part of her mind was always running a tactical scenario and trying to convince her brain not to put her in unnecessary danger. The briefest hint of hesitation meant she wasn't achieving the speed and momentum she needed to beat Lana and Aaron.

Tonight, she didn't care about falling. She risked that every time she hit her obstacle course in Warehouse One. No. It'd taken a while and many parkour runs before she finally realized the truth.

Parkour was just a type of exercise and movement to her, but that wasn't what it meant to Aaron, Lana, or the others. It wasn't what it had meant to the men who had created parkour.

Free-to-Move. It was right there in the name. Free as in

freedom. That was what most of the club members were striving for; a near-religious experience where they pushed their bodies to the limit and appreciated every single second as a fully-examined sensory experience.

Shay had started training in parkour as a tool at first, frustrated over her humiliation at the hands of Marcus. It was just like everything and everyone else in her life: something to make her more dangerous in her job. Joy had played little part.

As she caught a ledge from an office building across from the parking lot and pulled herself up, she understood that was no longer true. Like many other things in her life, things had changed.

Another quick pull moved her up, followed by another until she rolled onto the roof.

The occasional drone whirred past in the distance, but she didn't care, being too far from them for a good look. She'd just end up as Parkour Penny on the net again.

Shay allowed herself a grin as she launched from the edge of the building and caught a pipe on the next taller building. She shinnied up the pipe as she surveyed the grand glory of Los Angeles at night.

The city stretched out on all sides, an ocean of light and movement in the deepening darkness. From the top of a building at night, there was no detail to take in, just silhouettes. Enemies could be walking or driving beneath her, and people she'd never meet.

She didn't need to be concerned about a sniper or an assassin. With the cartel defeated and her criminal days moving farther and farther into the past, the sun might be able to shine on her dark life soon.

I'm hanging out at barbeques with cops now. Yeah, definitely getting softer. Ironic, considering my boyfriend's pretty much a living natural disaster and helped me destroy a cartel.

Freedom. Not fear.

Her new life had started because of fear and ennui. She didn't want to die in her kitchen, murdered by someone who could smile at her but didn't care about her. A couple years before she would have laughed at lecturing students and caring about people as absurd dreams or even signs of weakness.

Shay held no illusions that the parkour had changed her life. It'd taken time, effort, and new relationships, not to mention a death or five hundred. It was more that the activity was a nice symbol of her changed life.

The tomb raider launched herself onto the wood and steel skeleton of a high-rise office building. She caught a girder with her hands, and swung and caught the next, and then the next, like she was on the world's most dangerous set of monkey bars.

At the other side of the building, she released and flew straight toward another roof. She wasn't even sure how high up she was at this point. The lights of the cars were distant underneath here, more like dim fireflies than anything else.

A genuine smile lit her face.

What a damn cool way to tour the city.

More seconds blurred into minutes as Shay closed on the end of the course, her heart pounding and sweat soaking her clothes.

Almost there.

Shay jumped from a roof to a small balcony and immediately leaped from there to a ledge on the building on the opposite side. She swung a few times and jumped from the ledge to a canvas entrance arch in front of a deli and bounced off.

The tomb raider landed, her arms spread out on the middle of a sidewalk. Several curious people looked her way.

With a grin, she waved and sprinted off, not giving them time to process why the sky was raining women before Lana and Aaron arrived.

Shay risked a glance behind. She'd been so wrapped in the course she'd forgotten about them.

I still have the lead. I can do this. I can win.

The tomb raider cut into an alley, her eyes widening. A huge flat-nosed delivery truck was parked in the middle, blocking her path. She didn't understand why the driver had risked entry, given he had barely half a foot of clearance on either side.

Really, asshole?

Shay's gaze darted around the alley as she took in every stray protrusion. She pushed herself harder, her pounding feet echoing, and charged a frame-mounted row of lights over a door. She jumped toward the lights, hoping they could hold her weight, and pushed off the door and the frame.

The tomb raider flew to the top of the truck and ran across it. A delivery man emerged from another door behind the truck. He shook his head and looked up, wide-eyed, as Shay jumped off the truck's roof into a roll in the alley. Once she was back on her feet, she offered him a happy wave.

Two more quick corner turns, and three fences later, Shay stood in the parking lot of a frozen yogurt place, Sweet Storm.

She leaned over, her hands on her knees, trying to catch her breath. She hadn't pushed herself that hard without someone trying to kill her in a long time.

By the time she caught her breath and looked up, Aaron was jogging into the parking lot, Lana about five yards behind.

They slowed and stopped in front of Shay, also leaning over to catch their breath.

Lana wiped sweat from her brow. "Congratulations, Shay."

"Huh? What?"

"You beat both of us, not to mention everyone else."

Shay gave the other woman a broad grin. "Yeah, I guess I did."

Unburdened for most of the run even by worries over if the others were close behind, she'd finally done it. Her competitive soul had been satisfied because she'd taken first. She'd just had to start competing with herself instead of the others.

I'm damned good.

She shrugged. "The froyo's on me."

Shay nibbled on a slice of Peyton's latest creation, a mouth-watering sausage pizza with a touch of bacon. If he kept this up, he wouldn't just be Pizza King, he'd become Pizza Emperor. Not that she wanted to tell him that. Despite living under her stern eye and sharp tongue, the man's ego threatened to spill out of control—just like his sense of fashion.

Still, it was nice to have a little late-night snack that was so damn delicious. She'd gotten lucky that he was even still there so late.

The hacker was kneeling on the floor in front of Osiris. His ridiculous flared purple pants made her wonder if he was just going through a 70s phase. Whatever it was, she hoped that he'd cycle back to something less obnoxious soon. She wasn't a fashionista since a lifetime of violent and up-close killing had lowered its importance in her mind, but she still had certain basic standards.

People always claimed that fashion ran in cycles, not that she'd seen any of his recent outfits popular with anyone else. There still was plenty of time left in the 2030s. Maybe the decade would close out with a true revival of sartorial crimes long since forgotten.

Peyton pushed a small hollow ball with a bell toward Osiris. The cat meowed and knocked it back. They pushed the ball back and forth several times, the man smiling as if it were the most exciting thing he'd done that day.

Maybe I should get a pet. I can train my pet to threaten Osiris and keep him in line like I keep Peyton in line.

Let's see. Got a boyfriend, a protégé, and a daughter in all but name. Might as well complete the domestication set with a pet or two.

Shay snickered.

Maybe not. An attack falcon would be cool, though. Sky Shay.

Peyton frowned and looked up from his tabby. "Should I be scared?"

"What? I'm not allowed to think anything funny without telling you first?"

"Just saying, someone sitting there cackling without saying anything is kind of freaky. And that's just normal people, let alone you." He shrugged. "You're scary enough without cackling. If you ever lose it, I don't think even Brownstone could handle you."

Shay smirked. "I wasn't cackling. I was just thinking about getting a pet." She pointed at the cat. "I'm inspired by your cat. Maybe."

"A pet? You? Seriously?" Peyton frowned as if the idea were absurd inherently.

"Why not? If I can train a person, I can train a pet. The

only difference is that a pet is less mouthy and easier to bribe."

Peyton snorted. "If you believe that, you need to spend more time around cats."

"I don't need a cat. If I were to get a pet, I'd want something...I don't know, more tactical." Shay frowned and tried to run through the possibilities in her mind. She kept circling back to attack falcons or bears.

He laughed. "Don't think you can go to a pet store to get the kind of pet that would suit you, Shay."

"Oh? What do you think would suit me then, smart guy?"

Peyton shrugged. "I don't know. A shark with machine guns on the side? A Komodo dragon? Maybe a real dragon? You could ride him on jobs, machine guns optional."

"Don't tempt me. I can always check out Oriceran. Maybe I can find a spare dragon or two there."

Peyton rubbed his chin and pushed the ball toward Osiris. The cat pushed it back and meowed loudly.

"You know, a guard dragon *would* be pretty badass," the hacker agreed. "We should give him a name like Fluffy."

"Why would you name a dragon Fluffy?"

"Because it's funnier if the name's ironic. He'll be a huge guard dragon with scales, not some cute little thing."

Shay laughed. "Doesn't matter anyway. Not exactly like dragons are gonna let some random human tell them what to do. Don't meddle with them and all that."

"Raise it from an egg. It'll think you're its mommy."

She shrugged and shook her head, not sure how they'd ended up in this ridiculous discussion.

Maybe I can ask Alison what she knows about dragons. I'm sure they teach the kids about them at her school.

Peyton pushed the ball again to his pet, but the cat didn't bat the ball back. Instead, he lifted his head and pranced off. It was hard not to see it as anything other than haughty.

"Got a lot of other shit to get in order before I worry about pets," Shay commented. "Just fun to think about. Not everything's money and ass-kicking for me."

"Yeah, there's also Brownstone."

Shay rolled her eyes. "Okay, not everything's money, ass-kicking, or Brownstone for me."

Her phone chimed with a text, and she pulled it out of her pocket. She frowned. It was from her department head.

Need to speak with your immediately. Your career and the future of archaeology and revised history are at stake.

"What the hell?"

Peyton stood and dusted his pants with his hands. "Ass-kicking or money? Bad news? Somebody need to die?"

"Maybe. It's from my department head. He wants to talk to me right now." Shay shook her head. "I haven't talked to this guy outside of meetings all year, and suddenly he's stalking me on and off campus."

"Not like he knows where Warehouse Two is. You can just wait until you're on campus next. What's the worst thing he can do, fire you? That's not your real job."

Huh. What would happen if he tried to fire me? Still, what the hell does this message mean? The future of archaeology and history? Talk about being dramatic.

She stared at the message for a few more seconds. "No, something's wrong. My instincts are telling me so."

Peyton gave her an incredulous look. "Something wrong with some random professor? What, he got a really bad papercut, and he's bleeding out by the printer?"

"If you remember, with your help, I became a *random* professor, too." Shay shrugged. "Plus, this guy's interested in something that might have a link to Oriceran, which means there could be some serious artifacts involved. Not like idiots don't stumble upon random magic." She shook her head. "No. I'm going now, and I want you to run support, just in case it's some asshole I'm not expecting, like the Hollingsworth idiots or Yulia."

"Okay, you're the boss, but please tell me you're not going to have a gunfight at UCLA. You do that, we might not be able to cover it up."

"I'll just stick to knives then." She winked.

Peyton groaned.

***

"Just remember, this isn't a tomb raid," Peyton murmured through her earpiece. "And you're at a college. Even if it's nighttime, there are enough people there that if they hear any gunfire you will get swarmed with cops. If that happens, I'm guessing the little truce you have with that AET lieutenant will go away."

Shay rolled her eyes. "I did use to kill people for a living and not get caught. I do know a thing or two about sneaking around and avoiding cops."

She glanced back and forth as she approached the locked back entrance to the Fowler Annex. Dr. Weber's office was on the sixth floor of the red-brick building.

"Got anything on the drone?"

Peyton blew out a breath. "Nobody nearby, but internal cameras show people in a few of the labs plus a couple of janitors."

"Weber's office?"

He sighed. "Nope. No camera in there. The best I can do is the hallway. Nobody's there, though."

Shay pulled out her ID and swiped it on the lock. It clicked open, and she almost laughed. Her typical warehouse lock had multiple layers of security. It made the campus doors seem all but unlocked in comparison.

She pulled open the door and stepped into Fowler Annex. The entrance was dim, with only a few lights illuminating the area.

Shay glanced around, keeping her gun in its holster under her light jacket. As Peyton had said, this wasn't a tomb raid. Even if she didn't have an office in the building, she was a registered professor in the department and had every right to be there regardless of the time.

She made her way toward the elevator. "Anything?" she asked, her voice low. The throat-mic would pick up enough for transmission even if she were barely whispering. It was only habit that had her using a normal volume.

She pressed the UP button on the elevator.

"Nope. Nobody on the sixth floor from what I can see. You're home free."

The doors to the elevator opened, and Shay stepped inside and pressed the button for the sixth floor. She crossed her arms and frowned.

Peyton chuckled. "What are you going to do if you get there and he's just called you over to hit on you?"

Shay groaned and scrubbed a hand over her face. She hadn't even considered the possibility. Her instincts might be reacting to a whole different type of threat.

"I can be very intimidating," she mumbled. "And he'll end up regretting it."

"You do realize you can't pull a gun on your department head?"

"I can be very intimidating without a gun."

"You can't pull a knife either. Or break his arm."

Shay rolled her eyes. "I can handle it without violence." She frowned. "Pretty sure I can, at least." After a second she added, "We might need to pull the camera footage if I find a body in there."

"Then don't make a body."

She rolled her eyes. "I'm not saying I'll kill him, just that somebody else might."

"Okay, I'll pull an all-nighter if necessary," Peyton responded. "Though I'm awesome, so it won't take that long."

The elevator dinged, and the doors started sliding open. Shay reflexively rolled to the side and flattened herself against the wall.

No gunshots. No ice spears. No grenades. It was a good start to not dying.

Shay jogged toward Dr. Weber's office. Other than the

slight spookiness of a darkened hallway, there was nothing threatening.

She arrived at the office door and knocked. "Dr. Weber?"

No response.

She knocked louder. Again, no response.

Shay gripped her pistol and twisted the knob with her other hand.

The tomb raider threw open the door and stormed into the office, her gun out.

"What the hell?"

"What are you seeing?" Peyton asked.

Shay shook her head. Papers littered the office. His chairs were overturned, books all over the ground. Her stomach knotted at the sight of several older books with torn pages. His drawers had been pulled out, and their contents spilled all over. Even the computer was on its side.

That's not how you hack, dumbasses.

"Someone ransacked his office. They were obviously looking for something."

A large locked cupboard stood in the back. Several dents around the handle of the keyed lock suggested someone had been trying to open it.

"There's a locked cupboard in here. Wonder why they didn't open that? Maybe something spooked them, and they had to run. Maybe a security guard or a janitor."

Something rattled inside the stray piece of furniture.

Shay pulled out her gun. "Or maybe they *did* get inside."

"You see something?"

"I hear something," she whispered. She approached the

cupboard and reached into her pocket to pull out a paper-clip. Anyone else would have thought it was a random office supply, not realizing it was a gnome-crafted magical lockpick.

Does this count as evil purposes, Tubal-Cain? I'm trying to save my department head here.

Shay unfolded and slipped the lockpick into the lock. "*Open through will, open through heart, open through belief.*"

The door clicked open. She folded the lockpick up and put it back into her pocket. She raised her gun, took several deep breaths, and threw open the cupboard.

"Please," cried Dr. Weber. "I have a family." He cowered inside, hunched over. His arms were wrapped around him.

Shay blinked and stepped away. "You're in a cupboard." Her gaze dropped to her gun, and she slammed it back in her holster.

"Professor Carson?" The academic swallowed. "Why do you have a gun?"

"What the hell is going on?" Peyton all but shouted in her ear. "Who are you talking to?"

"I'm a woman, and it's LA at night, Dr. Weber."

She hoped Peyton would take the hint and shut up now that she'd used her department head's name.

"Oh, good point." Dr. Weber shook his head. "I shouldn't have sent that message. I'm sorry. I panicked, and I didn't even think about how risky it might have been for you."

Shay held out her hand and helped him out of the cupboard. "Well, I'm here now, and nobody else is, although they obviously were."

Dr. Weber took a moment to stretch before letting out a

long sigh. "I should have just called the police. I was fortunate that those ruffians didn't find me. I don't know why they left. They were speaking Spanish, and of the four languages I speak, Spanish isn't one of them."

"Okay, slow down a second. What the hell is going on?"

"I don't know. I was approached this morning by some ruffians in the parking lot. Gang members, I'm sure of it, with bandanas. They had skull tattoos on their faces. How distasteful. I assumed they were there to mug me, but they didn't ask for my wallet."

Shay nodded. "What did they ask for?"

"They wanted to verify that I was, well, *me*. Even claimed they had an interest in revised archaeology and history. They mentioned several papers I'd worked on, ones that are…no longer available, but they kept mispronouncing the site and artifact names. One man even mispronounced the word archaeology several times. Needless to say, I suspected something strange was going on. I managed to talk my way out of it, and I also suspect they didn't want to make a ruckus in broad daylight." He nodded to himself as if satisfied with his summary.

"Skull tattoos and bandanas?" Shay frowned. "That sounds a lot like the Demon Generals."

"What a distasteful name."

Shay snorted. "That's kind of the idea. They're a street gang in LA, decent-sized but not the kind of scum who might be interested in artifacts or history. At least not normally." She shook her head. "How the hell did you end up in a cupboard?"

"When I was heading to my car this evening, I spotted

them loitering in the parking lot." Dr. Weber sighed. "I fled back to my office."

"Why didn't you call the police?"

His cheeks reddened. "I dropped my phone when I was running back toward the building. It was right after I sent you the text."

Shay shook her head. "Why would you send me a text?"

She stared at him, wondering if he somehow knew about her true day job.

"One of the men mentioned the Anzick site. He mispronounced it, of course, but it was clear what he was interested in." He held up a hand. "Again, I apologize. It was wrong of me to get you involved."

"Well, I'm involved now, and something's really weird about this." Shay crossed her arms. "You mentioned old papers, ones that are no longer available?"

Dr. Weber nodded. "I told you about my earlier career. With the help of my mentors and even some aggressive EU law application, I actually managed to retract and cleanse the internet of my earlier shame. I maintained copies for my records, but I realized physical copies were too dangerous for my career, so the only thing left were computer backups."

Shay pointed with her thumb over her shoulder at his overturned computer at his desk. "I don't know if they tried to access the computer."

"I don't think they were looking for the computer." He reached into his pocket and pulled out a small black device with a tiny display and a silver panel. "I believe somehow they knew about this."

"A DNA-locked secondary authenticator." Shay's gaze

flicked from the device to the academic. "I'm guessing this gives you a code that lets you access where your papers are."

Dr. Weber nodded. "A few years back, I had a nice chat with a lovely fellow in IT who explained some of my security options for sensitive material. The backups of my papers are stored on an encrypted cloud service the university uses, but this is needed to access it."

Shay pulled out her phone to tap out a quick text to Peyton.

He's got an authenticator. Get ready to receive the code.

"Okay, I'm on it," Peyton responded in her earpiece.

The tomb raider held out her hand. "Let me see it for a second. Go ahead and authenticate."

Dr. Weber placed his thumb on the DNA scanner and then handed it to Shay. She tapped in the long authenticator sequence into her phone and sent it to Peyton.

The department head cleared his throat. "If I may ask, who are you texting?"

"A friend." She furrowed her brow. "A friend who knows James Brownstone. I figure maybe he can look into this for you. It's probably better than getting the cops involved. They'll ask a bunch of questions, and it'll look bad for the university."

Dr. Weber paled. "Oh, my. I hadn't thought of that. James Brownstone, though, as in *the* James Brownstone?"

"Scourge of Harriken, Granite Ghost, adopter of half-

Oriceran girls? Yeah, all that." She almost added Prince of Ab Town.

Shay was lying through her teeth. James might send the Brownstone Agency after the Demon Generals who had bounties, but he wasn't likely to want to get involved in the situation otherwise.

It didn't matter. She just needed a plausible lie to keep Weber from going to the cops and complicating things. She might need to dish out a little bloodshed later.

I'll let James know I'm borrowing his name a little later.

"I'm into his files and copying them now," Peyton reported.

Shay handed the authenticator back. "I'd go on vacation for a couple of days. Stay at a hotel. Clean this up so no one's too suspicious, and I'll have my friend get Mr. Brownstone to do what Mr. Brownstone does best."

Dr. Weber smirked a little. "Those ruffians will have swift justice delivered."

Swift justice? I care more about why some punk street gang is suddenly interested in magical artifacts. There's something more going on here, and I need to find out what.

Shay shrugged. "Yeah."

It's not as if no justice would be delivered. If a few Demon Generals died along the way, the world would be better off.

13

Peyton leaned against a lab wall, a smirk on his face. The place was interesting enough with rows of tables containing piles of electronics in various states of repair or construction, and a wall of shelves with about every sensor and meter known to man. He was sure the four computers on the opposite wall were connected to some ridiculous processing power.

I've got processor envy again, but there's something else way more important in this room.

Despite all the cool gadgets on display, the man's gaze kept drifting away from the technology to the slender neck and pretty face of his girlfriend.

How was I lucky enough to land a woman like her?

Amber turned from the table containing several small silver and black boxes with long black antennas to frown at him. "Are you even listening to me, Peyton?"

He nodded quickly. "Yeah, yeah, applying physics to communication in space. Those are prototypes for probes that they are talking about launching with the help of magic. Your part in this is to help with the code that does signal filtering."

"Okay, so you got all the main details right." She pursed her lips and crossed her arms. "But I still get the feeling you weren't listening."

"Even though I just explained everything you were doing?"

"Probably just listening to a few sentences here and there. Skimming, but with listening."

Peyton waved a hand. "Look, all the projects you're helping out with are cool and all, but you seem tense."

She lowered her glasses to eye him. "Huh? What do you mean?"

"Tense. You know…not relaxed." Peyton grinned. "And when a person is tense, they aren't going to be able to do their best thinking. Maybe that's what's distracting me, your tension. Yeah, definitely, it's your tension."

Amber pushed her glasses back up. "And how am I supposed to relax?"

His eyebrows lifted. "I've always wanted to make out in a lab. You know, passion near the final frontier of knowledge and truth. I'm sure you'd be very relaxed if we did something."

Amber scoffed, and her face grew scarlet. "We're not at either of our apartments. I think it's illegal to do that kind of thing in public."

"Make out, not have sex, and no one's even here." He nodded toward the door. "You told me no one would be here, and that was why you wanted to do the little tour now instead of later."

"Yeah, because I didn't want anyone giving you the

stink eye while I explained all this stuff." Amber shook her head. "Even if I *were* interested in making out with you, I can't because..." She sighed and gestured to his clothing. "Not when you're wearing that, of all things."

Peyton looked down at his red suit and frowned. "I thought you loved my fashion sense, and I love this suit. It's the perfect embodiment of Peyton style."

"Normally I do love your quirky choices, but when I was a kid, my grandma always made me watch this ancient kids' show called *Captain Kangaroo*. The host dressed like that, and...I can't make out with Captain Kangaroo. That's just too weird." She made a gagging sound.

Peyton winced.

Getting blocked by some old kids' show host. Of course. Just my luck.

"It was worth a shot." Peyton went to pick up one of the devices on the table to take a closer look. If he couldn't make out with his girlfriend, he might as well inspect the tech.

Amber slapped his hand. "Don't touch those. Do you have any idea how expensive they are?"

"Um, no? I'm guessing they cost more than a Snickers."

She rolled her eyes. "Well, they are really expensive. I'm not even sure I should have you in here, but I just thought you would find it cool. At least when you aren't obsessing over making out with me. Geeze. Men."

"What can I say? A beautiful nerdy woman around technology? It just puts me in the mood." He pointed at her. "You set me up."

Amber gave him a cool stare. "It's a nice line, but it still sounds like a line. So you don't care about interstellar communication because of your libido?"

I called her beautiful, but she's not budging. Better try to salvage this before she gets really pissed off.

"Interstellar communication is cool, yeah." Peyton forced a smile. "Even if I don't know all the details about it. Earth's more than enough challenge for me."

Amber's face brightened. "The real trick is that these receivers have to use such a wide frequency range. Because the project has funds for teleportation, that means they can put the probes directly into space without a rocket launch. Really darn far, as in AUs away. There has been some talk of actual light-year teleports, but apparently, it's hard to do that in space versus sending to Oriceran because of the lack of previous direct magical interaction. I don't understand all the details all that well." She waved a hand. "At a minimum, they can get a probe into orbit."

"Is that a lot cheaper than using a rocket? I mean, you have all those companies these days, and don't they compete on price? Half the funeral homes offer space burials now."

Amber nodded. "Yeah, it's not necessarily all that much cheaper, at least not with the project being charged for the magic. I don't quite get it. They can teleport stuff from Oriceran super-easy, but the minute we ask someone to put something in geosynchronous orbit, it's the most complicated spell in the world." She shrugged.

Peyton frowned. "If it's not cheaper, what's the advantage? Why bother?"

"The instruments don't have to survive the forces associated with a rocket launch, which means the team can get a lot more in terms of sensitivity. True broad-spectrum signal transmission and receiving, among other things."

He leaned toward one of the devices but kept his hands behind his back. "I'm not an expert on space communication, but isn't that kind of overkill? I mean, they know what frequencies they need to communicate with the probes, so who cares about trying to be able to transmit and receive everything? Receiving, I guess, if you're trying to do space exploration, but why transmission?"

Amber's mouth made a little O. "Because we don't know what potential frequencies a non-human or non-Oriceran intelligent civilization might be using. Signal attenuation due to the atmosphere is a killer, and if we want to have any chance of communicating with another technological civilization, our best bet is broad-spectrum transmission in space."

Peyton blinked several times as the gears in his brain finally turned. She'd been helping with research that could be applied to spacecraft and was now helping with research for probes that could communicate with aliens. A general pattern was emerging of a project to reach out and touch someone or something alien and non-Oriceran.

Are they just doing it because of scientific curiosity, or do they know more than anyone thinks?

Amber smiled. "There's a lot of interesting research, after all, about non-Oriceran extraterrestrials. People have spent a lot of time assuming every ancient alien thing was them, but now others are starting to question that." She shook her head. "It's strange how people kind of just almost forgot about the idea there could be life on other planets when we found out about Oriceran." She shook a finger. "If you think about it, the fact there are thousands of intelligent species over there only increases the chance that somewhere close to us, in our galaxy rather than a different dimension, is another planet with an intelligent species." She let out a sigh. "Even magic has its limits, especially at huge distances and when the magic users haven't dealt with the other planet directly, but if we combine magic and technology, we should be able to achieve the dream of extraterrestrial contact."

"You don't say?" Peyton forced a smile onto his face. "That's pretty intense. I didn't even realize you were involved in that kind of thing. That's crazy." He threw up a hand. "Crazy in a good way. I mean, it's awesome that you're involved in that kind of thing."

Self-control. I can't blurt out that I know all about the secret government projects that have already proven aliens exist. Even if it scored massive points with my girlfriend, Shay would put me into a probe and send me to the edge of the Solar System or use magic to drop me into some goblin garbage dump on Oriceran.

Amber nodded and rubbed her hands together. She looked around before leaning toward Peyton. "I know it sounds crazy, but some people think that there's non-Oriceran intelligent life on Earth right now. No one can prove it a hundred percent, though."

Aliens like James Brownstone.

"Interesting." He shrugged. "Considering all the weird stuff here, it doesn't really sound that crazy."

"You'd think so." Amber frowned. "But you'd be surprised how much pushback there is in academia over that kind of research."

Peyton chuckled a little and shrugged. "I find it funny

that in a world where we have to seriously worry about things like necromancers, people find the idea of a few little green men so out there. I mean, to me at least, discovering magic seems like a bigger deal than finding other guys who invented tools and nukes."

"I know." Amber shook her head and rolled her eyes. "That's the problem. Paradigms lock too easily. Everyone wants to pretend like they know the answers so they can look smart." She sighed. "Anyway, lot of people in the department doing a lot of interesting research, and maybe I shouldn't be telling you this, but I think they're closer to being able to prove some of this stuff than people think." She patted the edge of the table. "Which is why we're moving on to some of these more direct projects. If we know aliens are here, that makes contacting them either here or elsewhere just a matter of applied engineering, right?"

Peyton nodded slowly, keeping his breathing steady. He'd need to tell Shay all this later. When they'd discussed the spacecraft research that might link to vimanas she'd seemed more impressed than annoyed, but if the department were looking seriously into aliens, that might mean they'd end up stumbling onto the truth somehow about Brownstone.

The hacker didn't want to have to explain to his sometimes very angry, always gun-toting boss how his girlfriend had helped, even indirectly, bring down the government on her boyfriend.

Still, he wasn't sure if it'd actually be a problem. The general projects described seemed more about phoning ET at home, but there was still that risk.

Shit. Is this the end of my relationship? I lose out on my relationship because of her relationship? Better put on my background researcher hat. If I get some information Shay can use it'll be less of an issue, or we can do an even better job of protecting Brownstone.

Peyton cleared his throat. "I'm a nerd boy. I'd love to see some of this alien research. You know really dig into the papers and the data."

Amber sighed and looked away. "I really shouldn't have mentioned it. I've already told you too much, really. Look, I'd love to, and I'm sure eventually they'll publish it, but right now you don't have the clearance to look at the data or the initial reports."

"What do you mean, clearance? It's scientific research, not CIA spy plans."

"Most of our funding is from the government."

Peyton shrugged. "And how is that different from most research? Half the politicians complain about all the tax dollars being spent on research about stuff they don't understand. I wouldn't be surprised if the next election, someone's complaining about spending taxpayer dollars on looking for aliens."

Amber shook her head. "It's not run-of-the-mill NSF funding or anything like that. Lots of special DOE and DOD money. It's annoying. Lots of restrictions. No foreign nationals, which means no Oricerans or people who are too wrapped up in Oriceran stuff, which excludes a large chunk of the magic-using population. You know how hard it is to do magic-adjacent research with those kinds of limitations?"

Peyton stared down at the equipment covering the

table, his stomach tightening and a chill running down his spine. A government project that involved potential contact with extraterrestrials and had a high security clearance.

The temptation to poke around in the university systems to look for financial information rose, but he quickly quashed it.

It has to be Project Nephilim or Project Ragnarok funding. Probably. But I don't want to poke around and get them looking at Amber in a bad way. Given the kind of bullshit Durand was pulling, who knows what they might do to her if they got suspicious?

Just wonder why they want to chat with aliens but don't want anyone else to know. Seems mighty paranoid. Preparing to nuke someone we haven't even talked to yet? Even if they are here, maybe they are just working part-time at In-N-Out.

Peyton forced a smile onto his face. "Oh, well, we all have secrets."

———

Peyton blinked as he stared at Shay. He couldn't believe what he was hearing.

"You don't care?"

Shay shrugged. "No, I don't. Just don't tell her what we know and we'll be fine. Why did you think I'd care?"

"I don't know. I thought you'd be worried about Brownstone."

She snorted. "She's not the one who might go after Brownstone. If anything, she might be useful later on.

Time to go old-school spy. Seduce the target if necessary. Screw your way to useful information."

Peyton groaned. "Do you honestly not care, or is this just a thing where you think you can use her later?"

"Both." Shay shrugged. "Anyway, no, I don't give a shit if you keep getting sweaty in the sheets with the nerd girl. If it becomes a problem, we'll handle it."

Peyton nodded slowly, still surprised. He didn't have to dump his girlfriend. If anything, Shay was telling him to double down on their relationship.

She rolled her eyes. "And wipe that grin off your face. We've got more important shit to talk about than your girlfriend."

"Like what?"

"Weber's files."

A rooster crowed loudly from Peyton's computer.

No, no, no. Come on, Randy.

He frowned and spun toward the computer. His fingers flew across the keyboard, and then his jaw dropped.

Shay stepped into the office with a frown. "What's wrong?"

"Randy…" Peyton shook his head. He couldn't believe what he was seeing.

"What about your asshole brother?"

Peyton swallowed. "He's dead."

Shay arched a brow. "He's dead?" Peyton nodded. "That's convenient."

"Convenient? That's my brother you're talking about!"

She rolled her eyes. "Your brother who tried to have you killed. Your brother who kept after you even after we tried to Scrooge him. We had to screw up his finances to get him to stop because he was such a greedy fuck. So, yeah, I'm not mourning the loss of Randy 'Fratricide' Coolidge."

Peyton ran his hands through his hair. "Look, not saying he was a great guy. Just, it's a shock, you know?"

"What happened?"

"From what I can tell, some hitman said he set them up and got several of them killed. They took him out in revenge."

Shay clucked her tongue. "This is the problem when amateurs start rolling around in this shit. They don't know who they're dealing with, and they end up dead because they think they are big men."

"And you had nothing to do with this?"

She snorted. "I don't need hitmen to kill people for me. If I were gonna kill your brother, I would have walked up to him and stabbed him in the throat with a fucking knife. Being all cute about it is for pussies."

Peyton locked eyes with the tomb raider. Something about the whole thing smelled off. He wouldn't put it past Shay to set up his brother, but on the other hand, pursuing it wouldn't do any good. Randy was dead, and that was that.

Probably better that I don't know the total truth.

He blew out a breath. "I guess that's it, then. He's dead, and it's all over."

Shay nodded. "Yeah. This means you can start taking your life back. Maybe."

"Maybe?"

She grinned. "Right now, we still have those files to discuss."

Shay frowned as she took a corner in her Fiat.

Peyton's initial dive into Dr. Weber's files coupled with her efforts didn't reveal the kind of treasure she'd expect gang members to care about. They were typical archaeology papers, just with a few fanciful conclusions about the possible meanings of certain symbols and chemical analyses on the site. The only thing that stood out to Shay were some specific coordinates mentioned as possible portal entry-to-exit points.

Why the fuck would the Demon Generals give a shit about some old archaeology site? Even if there were artifacts there, it's not like they would be able to recover them, and they've never, ever shown interest in anything but petty street hustles and thug shit before.

Still, she didn't want to let it go. Despite what a lot of people thought, most criminals were both logical and lazy at the same time, especially common thugs. If the gang members were sniffing around Dr. Weber, it meant that for whatever reason, they thought there was something there of value.

Shay's phone rang, and she glanced at the screen in the middle of her dashboard. The miracle of Bluetooth pairing. She blinked at the number. Lily.

She switched to speakerphone as she stopped at a red light. "Lily?"

Someone panted at the other end, not talking.

"Lily, is that you?"

"It's me, Shay," the girl finally responded. "Sorry, I just had to catch my breath." There was some scratching, and when she next spoke, she sounded distant. "Is Casey okay? What? Use the potion then. Yeah, I know how expensive it is, but she might not make it if we take her to a hospital."

The light turned green, and Shay accelerated with a frown. "What the hell is going on?"

"Sorry, we were attacked. They came out of nowhere. We were barely able to hold them off, and a lot of people got hurt." Lily took a deep breath. "I need your help, Shay." Her voice trembled with rage.

Shay took a hard turn at the next intersection. She was going the wrong way if she had to go to the main nuclear tunnels entrance. "Was anybody killed?"

"No, a couple of people were banged up pretty badly, but everyone's alive. Casey took a bullet to the stomach, but it looks like the potion's working." She sighed. "I had a vision a minute before the attack, so we weren't taken totally by surprise, but it was too late to escape."

"Who were they?"

Lily sighed. "Don't know. They had all these stupid masks on, like Halloween masks."

Shay pulled onto an onramp. She needed to get to the tunnels faster than surface streets would allow. "What did they want?"

"Artifacts." Lily's breathing picked up. "They took my father's artifact from me, those sons of bitches. And a couple other things from other people."

"Shit. Okay, wizards then?"

"I don't think so. Didn't see any wands. A few of them had artifacts, like little things. One fired out little blue bolts, another was a ring with shields, but most of them just used guns, knives, or were punching and kicking people." Lily sucked in a deep breath. "I can't lose my father's artifact, not again. I don't care who they are. If I faced the witch, I can face these guys. I'll kill them if I have to."

Shay sighed. It wasn't all that long ago that some random homeless teens getting attacked wouldn't have fazed her. She would have pushed it away as not her business, but now there was only one response she could offer.

"I'll be right there, Lily. I'll help you find those assholes. We'll get your father's artifact back, and we'll make them pay, but don't do anything yourself. If you're dealing with violent thugs, you need a professional ass-kicker, and I just happen to know one who will be willing to help you for free."

Shay moved into the passing lane and accelerated. Too many things were unraveling at once. It was time for some situational triage.

She had no idea why the Demon Generals were poking around the college, but they'd failed to get what they wanted. The department head would be safe for a few days. The Anzick mystery would just have to wait until she helped her friend.

Huh. Yeah, that's what this is, helping a friend. It's a normal thing for most people, but still weird for me to wrap my mind around.

14

Shay stepped into the Great Treaty and made her way to the bar, ignoring the menagerie of Oricerans filling the bar and the bizarre layered dissonant chords coming over the speakers. The three-legged, three-armed creatures on the dance floor seemed to be enjoying the hell out of the song, though.

She was there for business. At this point in her career, she understood that it didn't matter how weird someone looked. In the end, all intelligent beings she'd dealt with seemed to operate from the same basic motivations.

Wings or tentacles don't erase greed or love. The Oricerans might have magic and some might live longer, but they aren't that different from us, for good or ill.

During her talk with Harry and Lily, she hadn't learned much more than she'd already been told. Someone had ambushed the kids, but the attackers seemed more concerned about artifacts, including threatening the kids while explicitly asking for specific ones.

The tomb raider's mind ticked away as she considered

what the slim evidence she had indicated. Everything would make sense if she put all the pieces together in the right way.

First, the assholes knew where the kids lived. That meant they had good intelligence or access to tracking magic. A lot of people don't even know about those teens.

Second, the assholes knew that some of the kids had artifacts, or at least knew they were magical and might have access to artifacts.

Three, they had enough discipline to jump a bunch at once and didn't care about using force against teenagers. From what Lily said, Casey would have been toast without the healing potion. That meant these assholes weren't Hollingsworth-style guys in it for the thrills, but seriously ruthless mercenaries or tomb raiders who don't care about killing innocent people.

Shay frowned and took a seat at the bar. The Kilomea bartender sauntered over and set a whiskey sour in front of her, and she looked up at him with an arched brow. She'd been thinking about that very drink on her way over and was still unsure if the bartender's ability to anticipate drinks was talent or supernatural.

I guess it doesn't matter as long as he gets the drink right.

The tomb raider picked up her glass and took a sip, enjoying the burn as it slid down her throat. A few more sips followed. A little alcohol to soothe her nerves wasn't a bad thing.

"Gnome's not here," the Kilomea rumbled. For a moment, his grinding voice reminded her of James. The frown on his face did, too.

"Not interested in Tubal-Cain, not today." Shay gulped some more of her drink. "Interested in talking with someone who can give me information about shit happening on the streets, artifact-related. Minor thefts and robberies."

"Lots of people can do that." He shrugged. "Why would they want to, though? Just because you've been in here a few times doesn't mean anyone trusts you."

Shay snorted. "Trust is overrated." She produced a nice stack of high-value bills from the pocket of her leather jacket and pushed it toward the Kilomea. "Figured you'd appreciate cash instead of something with an electronic trail."

The bartender pocketed the cash and nodded toward a corner table. A weathered-looking Wood Elf with a jagged scar running down his face sat there sipping some glowing blue concoction.

Shay took a moment to down the rest of her drink. "Thanks."

The Kilomea shook his head. "I'm just giving you a person to talk to. I don't guarantee anything. Be careful. That elf's not to be trusted, but he can give you good info."

She grinned. "I can be very persuasive."

With that, Shay hopped off the stool and walked over to the table. The elf looked up as she arrived, a thin frown on his face. The expression made his scar even more pronounced.

"Do I know you, human?"

She shrugged. "Shay Carson."

He chuckled. "Really, now?"

"Oh, so you *do* know me." She slipped into a seat across from him, not caring enough to ask for permission.

"I know of you. You can call me Carver." The Wood Elf

flicked his finger, and a thin whorl of his drink rose from his glass and went into his mouth. He swallowed. "Word on the street is that you're Brownstone's woman."

Huh? Is that the kind of shit they say?

Shay smirked, not wanting to show her surprise. She'd expected the Wood Elf to talk about how she was the famous and secretive tomb raider Aletheia, or, if not that, reveal that he knew about her dark past as a killer. About the last thing she'd ever anticipated was someone in the underworld hearing her name and just putting it together with James.

This means my cover's intact if even scumbags don't know who I really am. Nice to know.

Shay chuckled. "Yeah, James and I have fun together sometimes. What about him?"

The elf's face curled into a sneer. "That guy's fucking intense. Relentless, but fair."

"Fair?"

"Yeah." He shrugged. "I'm not an idiot. I've heard about the people he's taken out, but they were all assholes who didn't know when to stop. This city is filled with gangs and syndicates, both Oriceran and human. Brownstone doesn't fuck with most of them, because they don't fuck with him. Like I said, relentless but fair. Wouldn't want to run into him in a dark alley, but I respect his work."

Shay fished more bills out of her jacket and set them on the table. "Respect it enough that you'll take this little tip in exchange for some information?"

His gaze flicked between the money and Shay. She could almost smell the greed oozing off him.

Pointed ears and magic, or round ears and no magic. Money makes both worlds go around.

Carver shrugged, a slight smirk returning to his face. "Ask questions. I might have answers. Not guaranteeing shit, though."

"You familiar with the kids who live in the tunnels? The ones who are good at parkour."

He rubbed his chin. "Mostly half-breed trash from what I've heard. They have magic, but it's not reliable. They like to run around and steal, but I hear they've been lightening up on that lately. Good for them, otherwise they might end up getting killed when they take from the wrong person."

"Someone roughed them up earlier today." Shay leaned in, her face darkening. "Stole things from them; artifacts that were theirs."

"You know what they say. It's like I heard in a human song the other day—the wheel keeps on turning." He grinned.

The tomb raider snorted. "I just need to know who it was."

Carver eyed the money for a long while, running his tongue inside his cheek. "The Demon Generals."

Shay blinked. "What the fuck? Them again?"

"Again?"

"Don't worry about it." She waved a hand. "I just don't get why some punk street gang is suddenly executing lightning raids for artifacts. Something doesn't add up."

"Haven't you heard? They're under new management."

Shay frowned. "New management?"

Carver grinned. "Remember the Nuevo Gulf Cartel?"

Shay's stomach tightened. "From what I heard, they're

done. Someone raided a big meeting of them, killing all the leaders. They then hunted down the rest. After that, they were in complete chaos, and other criminal groups and law enforcement dismembered them. They don't exist anymore, not really."

"Yeah, that's all true, but it's not like every last guy in the cartel was killed. Just all the leadership. More than a few talented foot soldiers survived. They couldn't save their cartel, but they've been working for a serious professional criminal organization and have experience. Some of them melted into other cartels, but some of them are taking their chance to be a big man in a smaller group."

She blew out a breath. "So, some ex-cartel douchebag is trying to turn the Demon Generals into an artifact-smuggling group?"

"Among other things. It's a guy calling himself Tío."

"Tío? As in uncle?"

Carver shrugged. "He picked the name, not me. He's pushing artifacts, weapons, and drugs. High-end distribution, not petty local shit. I think the guy's being a little too aggressive, but I can't argue with his results so far. Without the Nuevo in town, there are still a lot of opportunities to expand territory, and some of the newer arrivals, like the 25K, don't know this city like the Demon Generals do, so with good leadership, they might become a serious threat."

"Do they have some sort of warehouse where they store artifacts? They've just grabbed the shit, so I doubt they've had time to move it."

Carver laughed. "You planning to take on an entire gang?"

"Not if don't have to, but they stole something from a

friend of mine. There's a reason I'm with Brownstone. We both don't tolerate people fucking with us or our friends."

The Wood Elf arched a brow. "I know they have a big deal going down in a couple of days at the ARCO Tower. They're planning to sell stuff off to the highest bidder. If you want a chance to get your friend's shit back, that's your best bet." He shrugged. "But that's going to be very heavily guarded. Demon Generals, and I hear the buyer is Russian Mafia."

Shay blew out a breath and stood. "Good to know."

"Your funeral if you go. Don't say I didn't warn you."

I have a little planning to do. We need to hit that place tomorrow before everybody and their fucking mother is there.

15

Shay leaned against her Fiat as she waited for Lily to emerge from the tunnel. She'd explained the plan to raid ARCO Tower over the phone the previous night, and the girl seemed more than a little enthusiastic. Blood-thirsty, really.

Not that I can blame her. Those assholes took the last link she has to her dad. They'll only get what's coming to them.

The tomb raider frowned as two people emerged from the huge pipe in front of her—Lily and Harry. She pushed away from the car and marched toward them. This was the time for professional ass-kicking, not tunnel rat improv.

Shay looked at them and crossed her arms, waiting for Lily to explain why Harry was with her.

Lily sighed. "Harry wants to come."

Shay snorted. "No way in hell."

He frowned. "It's not just Lily's stuff that got taken. I've got a responsibility to help get it all back. I'm the leader."

Shay shook her head. "This isn't going to be a running-around-at-night-trying-to-avoid-some-beat-cops   deal.

This is going to be a careful infiltration into a guarded tower. If everything goes well, it'll be easy, but if it goes badly, there's gonna be a lot of shooting and dying."

Harry narrowed his eyes. "You don't think I have what it takes?"

"I don't know if you have what it takes. Frankly, I don't give a damn if you do." Shay shook her head. "I only go on jobs with people I trust with my life."

Harry nodded toward Lily. "She can vouch for me, and it's not like you haven't seen me on my feet in a dangerous situation."

"That's not how this works. I don't know you well enough to know how you'll react when bullets start flying, or you take a hit. At least with Lily, I know she's received enough training and learned the right lessons that I won't have to distract myself keeping an eye on her. This shit is simple. Either you stay, or neither of you goes. I'm going either way, but this isn't a babysitting job."

The boy frowned and looked at Lily. "Aren't you going to say something?"

Lily sighed and averted her gaze. "Maybe she's right, Harry."

He blinked. "What? How can you say that?"

"It's just, I couldn't forgive myself if something happened to you. I just keep thinking back to Casey and all that blood."

Harry frowned. "Nothing's going to happen to me."

Lily took a deep breath. "I've already seen some strange and dangerous stuff in my time with Shay. I know she can take care of herself as long as I don't mess things up, and it doesn't matter anyway. There's nothing I could say to convince her to let you come, so either you stay, or I can't go." She shrugged.

Shay nodded. "Exactly."

Harry looked at the women for a moment, a deep frown on his face. "Damn it. This isn't fair."

The tomb raider snorted. "Harry, you of all people should know that life isn't fair." She nodded toward the car. "Lily, your tactical harness is loaded up and in your seat. Come on, we have some ass to kick and some artifacts to recover."

Shay and Lily emerged from the entrance to a parking garage across the street from the ARCO Tower. The thirty-three-story office tower pierced the night sky above them. It was a clear night, the stars and moon making it brighter than Shay would have liked for a night operation.

"From what Peyton found out," Shay explained, "all the artifacts stolen from the tunnels are being stored on the thirtieth floor." She patted her back to make sure her pack was secure, then checked her junior partner's.

We might be able to pull this off without having to even shoot anyone.

Shay snorted.

Yeah, right.

Lily frowned. "What?"

"Don't worry about it, kid. Just me being cynical."

Lily looked around and frowned. "Still confused about some of the plan. Why didn't we just enter from the top?"

"It'll be easier to go up and then go up a little more to

escape than the opposite." Shay blew out a breath. "Which means we're gonna have to stick to the plan. Floor entry to make our way up to the thirtieth floor to find the artifacts."

A savage smile appeared on Lily's face. "As long as I get my father's artifact back, I don't care what we have to do."

"We'll get it, Lily. Just have to be smart about it. The guards on the lower levels are just rent-a-cops, but once we get to the thirtieth floor, we risk running into gangsters and Mafia. Luckily, there's only a few there. That'll make certain things simpler if we have to get rough." She shot at a glance at the girl. "Seeing anything?"

Lily shook her head. "Nope."

Shay grinned. "At least you're not seeing us get shot. Peyton, what's the camera and alarm situation?"

"I've got the camera feed to them looped now," he reported through her earpiece. "Should have a good hour before anyone notices. All external alarms have been disabled. They're all alone."

"Guess it's showtime." Shay jogged across the street, Lily close behind. She slowed as she hit the sidewalk in front of the building and tossed Lily her magical lockpick. "Don't lose that."

"I won't. You know this looks totally lame. It's just a paperclip."

Shay smirked. "It gets the job done. Now you do the same."

Lily clenched and unclenched her hands a few times before jogging toward the massive glass entry doors.

The magical lockpick made quick work of the doors. Lily rushed inside and started running around and waving her hands. She shouted at the top of her lungs, although

Shay couldn't hear it through the closed doors. Thankfully, the girl had deactivated her microphone.

Just don't get caught, kid, and this will be easy.

Lily disappeared from sight and Shay flattened herself against an outside wall, awaiting Peyton's signal before making her entry. The timing on this might be tighter than she liked, but if the enemy was tipped off too soon, they might realize what they were targeting.

Her heart rate kicked up as the seconds ticked away. She'd still not gotten that used to joint operations with anyone but James, and he wasn't the kind of man you had to worry about.

Did I just get Lily killed? Those might not be gang members or mobsters, but they do have guns, and they might be trigger-happy. Great reflexes can only do so much to save you from bullets.

"You need to move now," Peyton's voice crackled over the comm. "She's got all the first-floor security guys on the opposite side of the building. They tried to call the police, but I blocked the call."

Shay burst away from the wall toward the unlocked glass doors. She threw one open and rushed straight toward the elevator. Hiking up thirty flights of stairs and then taking on dozens of enforcers wasn't a good strategy. It was time for a little laziness with the aid of technology.

She hit the UP button and waited, shifting from foot to foot and looking behind her. Painful seconds later, the elevator dinged, and the doors opened. The tomb raider stepped inside and pressed the button for the thirtieth floor.

"How are you doing, Lily?" Shay asked.

No response. Her stomach knotted. She could have just forgotten to turn her mic on.

"Lily? Turn your mic back on."

"She's fine," Peyton reported. "She turned it back on, but there's something wrong with the transmission. She's shaken all the guards."

Shay let out a sigh of relief. "Good."

"Shit. Something's wrong."

"What do you mean, something's wrong?" Shay gritted her teeth.

"I lost all the camera feeds. I think someone disabled all the cameras from inside the building. That means I don't get the feed, but neither do they, even with the looping. Don't worry, we're still blocking their phone lines and the cell phone frequencies. If they aren't using this frequency to transmit, they're not talking to anyone."

Shay stared at the floor number display as it ticked up. "They might be spooked by the intruder report. What was the last thing you saw?"

"A few gang members with tattoos, and a couple of guys in suits. Just a few of them."

"No surprise there. Tío?"

"One sec."

Shay pulled out her gun to give it a quick check and then reached inside to verify that her adamantine knives were in their sheaths. Tonight she anticipated rivers of blood if she ran into anyone.

Demon Generals and Russian Mafia weren't like the thrill seekers of Hollingsworth. They were ruthless killers, but she'd show them what a real ruthless killer was like.

Huh. Guess it's a good thing I don't have any pets after all.

Some asshole would probably end up killing my cat, and I'd have to go all James all over them and kill half of LA.

Shay smirked.

"Yeah," Peyton finally responded. "I ran some quick facial recognition on the previous footage. Ninety-five-percent chance he's one of the guys in the suits."

"Good. I don't like the idea of even a fragment of the Nuevo Gulf Cartel still being around. I'm not gonna go out of my way to find him, but if I run into him, I'll say hi with a little lead." Shay glared into the smooth, reflective metal of the closed elevator door.

The elevator abruptly stopped on the twenty-fifth floor.

"What the hell? Why did the elevator stop?"

Peyton sighed. "Looks like they figured it out. I'm keeping the door closed for now, but I can't do much if they force it open."

"Any guys near me?"

"Nope, not yet. They're having to take another elevator."

Shay grinned. "Looks like it's time for Plan B. Go ahead and open it."

"You sure?"

"Yeah. Five flights of stairs I can handle."

Peyton chuckled. "I guess this is why I don't go into the field. Too much running. It's tiring just listening to you."

The elevator doors dinged and slid open. Shay ran around the corner and threw open the door to the stairwell.

She stopped for a moment to listen for footsteps or shouting but heard nothing. With a smile, she started taking the stairs two at a time. Shay arrived at the thirtieth floor and peeked through the narrow window. Without active camera coverage, she had no idea where anyone might be, but she'd memorized the layout of the floor and three likely storage rooms where they might be keeping artifacts prior to sale.

Shay removed her 9mm from her holster, then reached into another pouch on her tactical harness and retrieved her magical silencer. After screwing it onto the weapon, she slowly pulled the door open.

She entered the thirtieth floor. No one so far. She hurried down the hallway and took a corner. Two men with skull tattoos stood on either side of a conference room door. Demon Generals.

One of them blinked. "Who the fuck are you?"

Shay whipped up her gun and put a round in his head, then another in his friend's. They slumped to the ground, their blood splattered against the wall. The magical silencer had made the shots mere hisses.

Poor discipline.

She walked over to the door they had been guarding and waited a few seconds. She gave herself a three-count and kicked open the door.

A long polished wood conference table sat in the center of the room, a perimeter formed by leather chairs. A familiar piece of metal had been placed under a glass dome: Lily's artifact. Two others, a small brush and a ring, she didn't recognize but assumed they were from one of the other teens.

"So much for the storage rooms," Shay mumbled. "I found Lily's artifact."

"Lily should be there soon," Peyton reported. "I spotted

her running up the stairwell before I lost cameras. She's coming in from the opposite side, it looks like."

"Good. This is being damned easy. Glad we caught these assholes by surprise. I'll catch up with her." Shay yanked off the glass domes, then grabbed the three artifacts and stuffed them into pouches in her tactical harness.

Shay stepped out of the conference room, taking a moment to glance down at the dead gang members before jogging down the hallway. Voices in Russian drifted from around the corner.

She flattened herself against the wall and crept down the rest of the hallway before a quick peek around the corner. Two men in dark suits sat there chatting and gesticulating wildly, clearly agitated. Large bulges in their jackets outlined their not so-concealed weapons.

Shay spun into the hallway and put both men down before they'd even realized what was happening. She continued toward the second stairwell. The door opened, and Lily stepped through, panting.

Lily looked at Shay, fear in her gray eyes. "We're screwed."

The tomb raider shook her head. "No, we're doing great, kid. I grabbed the artifacts. We just have to complete the exit plan, and we're good."

"You don't understand." The teen swallowed. "I just had a vision. Tons of guys are coming. Demon Generals and Mafia from the looks of it."

"Peyton? Lily said she just had a vision of reinforcements. What the hell? I thought you said they couldn't communicate."

Peyton groaned. "Yeah, one of the drones just spotted a bunch of SUVs and cars on the way, coming damned fast."

"How many vehicles?"

"Enough that I think you'll run out of ammo if you tried to take on all those guys." Peyton sighed. "There's no way they got a message through. I was even monitoring our frequency for other encrypted traffic."

Shay frowned and shook her head. "Then they somehow knew we were gonna raid tonight. Maybe one of the tunnel kids ratted us out."

Lily glared at her. "None of them would sell us out."

Shay shrugged. "Just considering the options. If not… Shit." She scrubbed a hand down her face. "That damned elf must have placed a phone call. He was playing both sides. Doesn't matter now. We stick to the plan and get the hell out of here from above."

She rushed past Lily into the stairwell, and the teen spun on her heel to follow. They all but flew up the last few flights.

The tomb raider reached for the roof door, but Lily jumped and pulled Shay down.

"What the hell are—" the tomb raider began.

Bullets ripped through the roof access double doors. A dozen holes decorated both doors a moment later.

"Oh." Shay blinked. "Good vision timing there."

Lily grinned. "I try."

"Stay low. Can you tell me what we've got?"

The teen took a deep breath. "Four guys, three on the left and one on the right."

Time to do this. They don't have their reinforcements yet.

"Okay, stay low." Shay crept over to the door and reloaded. "One…two…three." She threw open the door.

The crack of pistols and rifles echoed in the night. Bullets whizzed over her head. Two Demon Generals stood on the left, both with handguns, and one tall Russian mobster holding a rifle. A smiling man in an expensive suit stood on the right with a rifle in hand.

Shay didn't give herself time to register any other details before she jerked her pistol up and snapped off two shots at the first man on the left. Three quick moves of her hand and shots later, all four lay on the ground.

She stood and rushed toward the groaning men. Without any hesitation, she put bullets in their heads.

Lily blinked a few times at the dead men. "Wow."

"This is what it means sometimes, kid. Always keep that in mind." Shay shrugged. "Not gonna shed any tears for Demon Generals and mobster trash." She stared down at the man in the expensive suit. Nothing was getting all those stains out. "Tío. Guess his little new mini-cartel plans are already over, and the Demon Generals can go back to being worthless street trash."

I won't let any speck of the Nuevo Gulf Cartel ever rise again.

Shay shook her head and glanced around. Despite all the violence and blood, they now stood atop a 33-story building that provided a wonderful view of the panorama of the city at night. From this height, the lights all joined together, an almost hypnotic rendering of a cityscape.

"Everything okay?" Peyton asked.

"Yeah. We're both fine. The reinforcements here yet?"

"Almost. A couple of minutes."

Shay snorted. "Too slow. We can catch our breath."

A dark shadow in the distance caught her attention, and concern swallowed the wonder.

"Shit. What now?" She pulled binoculars from her backpack and looked toward the movement.

It was no Ice Witch looking to steal from her or flying gangster reinforcements. It was a man swinging from the top of City National Tower. A man she recognized, even in the darkness, his face burned into her soul.

Marcus, you son of a bitch. Of course, the one time I run into you, you're too far away for a rematch.

Shay shook her head as the thief leaped off his line, falling backward before snapping his arm up to catch a flagpole and spinning around several times. He released the pole and flew upward, where he caught the edge of another roof one-handed.

The timing was exquisite. Even the smallest miscalculation would have sent him plummeting to the street below.

"It's like the guy thinks he can't fall. Like he doesn't give a shit in the world. He's just…free to move. No cares, no worries."

Lily moved to Shay's side and watched Marcus. "That's insane. No one from the tunnels would try something like that at the distance he just swung and jumped. So *that's* what it's supposed to look like."

The tomb raider looked at the girl with an arched eyebrow. A strong wind cut over their roof, their hair fluttering in the wind.

Shay burst out laughing. Lily blinked and looked at Shay, a confused look on her face.

There'd been so much blood even after Shay had left

behind killing. Every moment had been a struggle with her assuming her next encounter might cost her life. She'd told herself that she had a life plan, but all she'd had was a vague idea to make money. She wasn't sure if she expected to live as long as she had.

James had changed that. Alison had changed that. Now Lily had changed that, too.

Shay finally realized what she'd lacked before. All animals might want to live, but not all animals had a *reason* to live.

I should have died so many times, but I haven't. And I'm just glad to still be alive and have a reason for it.

She laughed harder. Gratitude. What a novel feeling.

"It's a great night to be alive, Lily," Shay explained. "Maybe every night's a great night, but I'm really feeling it this night." She threw her head back and howled at the moon.

Lily's eyes widened, and then she threw her own head back to join her mentor.

They howled over the course of a half a minute before stopping and grinning at each other.

They heard shifters in the distance howling back.

Shay and Lily laughed hard.

"Um, I have no idea what you're doing right now," Peyton reported, "but the reinforcements are at the front. So, maybe stop being crazy and get the hell out of there."

Shay chuckled and shook her head. She reached into her backpack to pull out a grappling gun, then nodded to Lily. The girl pulled one out of her backpack.

"We got what we came for." Shay spared another quick glance at the dead Tío. "And I've nipped a problem in the bud. The Demon Generals won't be bothering my department head anymore. Still wonder what their new boss wanted from him, though." She walked to the edge to aim the gun at the roof of a parking garage below them. "For now, let's get the hell out of here."

16

Shay smiled and tapped her foot. It hadn't been that hard to track down Carver. He lived in a run-down apartment building in Elf Town, which suggested his information brokering wasn't as lucrative as she might have expected. A little early-morning visit wasn't out of order, and people would probably wait to call the cops if he ended up screaming for whatever reason.

Don't know why this guy lives in such a shitty place. The asshole took money from me and from the other guys. He should be living in a mansion if he does that kind of double-dealing all the time.

She lifted her hand and knocked lightly. It didn't take that long before the door opened. The elf's eyes widened. He hadn't been expecting her, probably for more than one reason.

"Hey, Shay," he mumbled. "Didn't know you knew where I live."

"You'd be surprised what I can find out." She shrugged.

"May I come in?" she asked, her voice full of forced sweetness.

"Sure, sure." He swallowed and motioned inside.

Shay stepped inside, and he closed the door behind her.

Carver stepped back. "How did your—"

The tomb raider had an adamantine knife out and at his neck before he could even blink.

"So, funny thing happened the other day. Despite the fact that I'd disabled the alarms, communications, and all of that kind of shit, a bunch of reinforcements showed up. Fortunately, I got away before they could get to me, but it really got me to thinking." She slowly moved the knife up and down but kept it as his neck. "What if someone sold me out? That led me to my second question: *Who* sold me out?"

Carver gritted his teeth. "I wouldn't sell you out. I told you before, I don't want to be on Brownstone's bad side."

Shay chuckled. "Now the problem isn't that you're on his bad side. It's that you're on *my* bad side, asshole. Brownstone's a saint compared to me."

"I don't know what you're talking about. I didn't sell you out."

She narrowed her eyes. "Don't bother playing dumb. I already know you received a big deposit in your account the other day from a shell company owned by our mutual friend, the recently deceased Tío. This is why a scumbag like you should always do business in cash." She winked and lowered her knife.

"You're not going to kill me?" Carver rubbed his neck, his face a mask of surprise.

"Let's just say I had a recent epiphany that makes me

slightly less bloodthirsty. Plus now you fucking owe me, asshole, and if I ever end up dead, a nice little automated message will go to one James Brownstone about how you might be involved. Then you get to see what the Scourge of Harriken does to one single elf."

His eyes widened. "Hey, that's not fair."

Shay shrugged. "Let's just say it's my way of keeping you honest. And don't worry, if I ever die, James won't kill only one person. Think about all the people he killed when his dog died. I think a *country* might disappear during his revenge over me." She waved and sheathed the knife. "See you, Carver."

She opened the door and stepped out, sparing one last glance for the pale elf. He dropped to his knees, his breathing heavy.

"I have to make sure you never die," he mumbled.

Shay yawned as she stepped out of her car. It'd been a long night, and she'd gotten up far too early. Lily hopped out of the passenger's seat. She'd stayed the night in the tunnels, but the tomb raider had suggested they train together in the morning at Warehouse One.

Lily wanted to anyway, even if Shay had an ulterior motive.

The girl took several steps, then stopped to blink at a waving Alison in the middle of Warehouse One. "Huh?"

"I'm Alison."

Lily looked at Shay, and the tomb raider offered a shrug and a smirk.

"Um, I'm Lily. Nice to meet you."

Shay cleared her throat. "Alison Brownstone, my boyfriend's adopted daughter."

The Gray Elf teen nodded quickly. "Yeah, I…kind of knew all that. It's just weird to see her here."

Alison laughed. "I knew Shay before you did, and I asked to meet you."

Lily frowned. "Why? I don't even know you."

"That's the problem. You don't know me, and I don't know you."

"Not following."

Alison shrugged. "Anyone Aunt Shay's spending a lot of time around is a person worth getting to know. It means you're worth spending time around. She doesn't waste her time." She offered a hand. "I know we've just met, but I'm sure we could be good friends."

Lily swallowed, her cheeks reddening. "Oh, sure." She shook her head. "Nothing against you, Alison, but like you said, you don't know me. Maybe I'm not the good person you think I am. Maybe I'm not worth getting to know."

Trying your cynical-girl-off-the-street routine, Lily. Trust me, I've tried that one on her.

Alison laughed.

Yeah, here it comes. One of them can see the future, and the other one can see souls.

"Shay hasn't told you a lot about me, has she?" Alison asked. "About the kinds of things I can do."

Lily shrugged. "Not really."

"I see souls."

"Huh?"

Alison grinned. "I can see the energy and souls. I can

tell what people are feeling, if they're lying, that sort of thing. I can see your soul, and it's the beautiful soul of a good person. So you can tell me you're a bad person if you want, but I won't believe it."

Shay snorted. "Don't let her mess with your head too much, Lily. She does that kind of thing to James and me all the time; really gets into your head. Makes you question yourself."

"Oh, Aunt Shay, don't be that way."

Lily laughed. "Aunt Shay? It's so weird to hear her called that."

"I'd prefer if she were my mom, but we're still working up to that."

Shay blinked several times, then laughed. "Don't marry me off just yet, kid. I'm still young."

"Just saying."

The tomb raider clapped her hands. "Now that introductions are out of the way, why don't we do what we all came here to do? Train."

Lily and Alison nodded.

She pointed to the climbing wall that marked the beginning of her current basic obstacle course. She'd simplified some of the obstacles and their positions so Alison would have a better chance and excluded some of the difficult strength obstacles, but it was still a challenging course.

"Why don't you two see who's better?" Shay suggested

Lily smirked. "Not to brag, but you have been training me."

Alison scoffed. "And I've been getting training from both Aunt Shay and my dad, who's the Scourge of Harriken, by the way."

The other girl grinned. "Less talk, more walk." She jogged toward the climbing wall.

Alison hurried after her. She raised her hand and sent out a magical pulse.

Lily blinked and looked over her shoulder. She glanced at Shay, but the tomb raider did nothing but smile.

You figure it out, Lily. You're magical, so it should be easier for you.

Both girls hit the climbing wall and scrambled up it. A few minutes and several more pulses later, both girls were scrambling down a net, panting, with sweat pouring down their faces.

When they hit the bottom of the net, Lily frowned. "Alison, wait."

Alison took a few more steps before stopping to look over her shoulder. "Ready to concede to my greatness already? That didn't take long." She took a few deep breaths. She was pretty winded too.

"You're crazy, you know that?"

Shay crossed her arms and smirked.

Finally figured it out, did you, Lily?

"Why do you say that?" Alison asked. "Not saying I'm not crazy, just wondering why you think I am." She completed her sentence with a merry grin.

"You can see souls, but you can't see much else, can you?" Lily shook her head. "You're blind. It's weird, though. I can kind of see it when you move, but other times, it's like you're suddenly not blind."

Alison shrugged. "I can see magical energy now thanks to the training I'm getting at my school."

Lily frowned. "Is that why you're sending out the pulses? So you can kind of see the magic on stuff?"

"Yeah. Why did you think?"

"First I thought you were just trying to distract me, but Shay didn't say anything, so I figured there had to be more to it." Lily stared at Alison open-mouthed for a few seconds. "I can't believe you're running an obstacle course blind."

Alison laughed. "It's not the seeing that's the hard part. Dad and Aunt Shay were running me so hard when I first came home on summer vacation I was throwing up."

Lily snickered. "That sounds like Shay."

The tomb raider rolled her eyes. "Technically, her dad made her throw up. I pushed her to her limits, but there wasn't as much vomiting involved."

"Yeah, you are good at pushing people."

Alison wiped a little sweat from her forehead. "Intense exercise that might end with someone throwing up? I guess in this family that's how we get to know each other."

Lily blinked several times, looking more than a little startled.

It was the word family that did it, wasn't it?

Shay didn't say anything else, just letting the teen take it in. Maybe, just maybe, they could have something more than a mentor-and-protégé relationship.

All those years of thinking I didn't need anyone, and now I might end up with not only one but two daughters.

Shit, what am I saying? Daughters? I'm not a mom. I'm the cool aunt who can kick ass and paraglides off mesas.

She snickered.

Lily eyed Shay. "It's very creepy when you do that without saying anything first."

"You been talking to Peyton?"

Alison stretched her arms above her head. "I think I'm going to go hit the showers."

Lily sniffed her armpit. "Yeah, I could use a shower myself."

Shay nodded, and the girls set off toward the hallway leading to the shower.

"You said you learned to see magical energies at your school?" Lily asked.

Alison nodded. "It's not so much they were trying to teach it to me as the more magic I learned, the more I could see."

"So you go to magic school?"

"Yeah. The School of Necessary Magic. It's in Virginia. Everyone there is like us—special."

Shay smiled as the two girls disappeared down the hallway talking about the school, relief spreading through her over a worry she hadn't even realized she had.

Lily and Alison were the ultimate examples of compartmentalized parts of her life. Shay had half-worried that if the girls were to meet, they'd hate each other, being similar in that they were both stubborn magical teenagers.

So much for compartmentalizing my life. Everything's kind of blurring together lately, but I'm not so sure that's bad. It's making things less stressful, not more.

Shay crossed her arms. Somewhere along the way, she'd stopped merely existing and started living. And damn it, she liked the feeling.

Alison laughed. "So when Izzie came and asked me, I said, 'Why are you asking me? I'm blind, remember?'"

Lily laughed. "Even after all these years, Harry thinks it's funny to come to me after something happens, or he wins in a game and say, 'What? Didn't you see that coming?'"

The teens giggled.

Fifteen minutes into their drive from Warehouse One to Warehouse Two, Shay was struck by two things.

First, the girls got along great. It was like they were long-lost sisters. Even if Alison had been spoiled by James, that didn't change the fact that she'd had a hard life and had lost her mother in a depraved act of betrayal. Both girls had experienced the darker sides of life too young. Even though neither was talking about those depressing topics, it was almost as if they could sense that pain in the other lurking just below the surface and it formed a natural bond.

The other striking thing about the conversation was that Shay was sure she'd never heard Lily talk so much on so many topics. This wasn't a quick quip and then an escape, but a detailed far-ranging discussion. Even when they'd spent hours alone together on tomb raids, the girl hadn't talked this much.

Does she talk like this with the tunnel kids? At the end of the day, I'm her scary mentor, not another one of the girls.

Shay smiled. Yes, she'd exposed Lily to violence and death, but the girl's whole life had been that. The tomb raider was just giving her the tools to thrive in a world that wasn't always nice.

Unfortunately, any adult who has been subjected to a constant barrage of teenagers chatting away soon reaches their limit, and Shay was no exception.

She rolled down her window, enjoying the breeze and the natural white noise provided by the air rushing into the car.

Another few minutes passed when her phone announced a call from Peyton. She grabbed her earpiece and stuck it in her ear before turning it on and answering.

"What's up?"

"I've got a job. It pays a little less than you normally ask, but it's also so easy that I figured, why the hell not?"

Shay chuckles. "Let me hear it first."

"Know the Paisley Caves in Oregon?"

She furrowed her brow in thought. "Nope, but I already like that this job is stateside."

"Exactly." Excitement colored Peyton's voice. "Four caves in an arid, desolate part of Oregon north of the city of Paisley. About 4,500 feet up, geologically lots of it volcanic rock. Caves were carved by waves from the nearby Summer Lake during the last Ice Age."

Some of her interest faded. "Okay, the geology lesson's nice, but why do I give a shit about some caves in Oregon?"

"One of the caves may contain evidence of the oldest human presence in North America. But, in terms of the job, there are supposed to be three gold figurines hidden in the cave that might provide evidence of contact between the humans of that area and Oricerans."

"Interesting." Shay changed lanes. It wouldn't be that

much longer until they arrived at Warehouse Two. "Magical figurines?"

The two girls in the back continued chatting, not even realizing Shay had taken a call.

"As far as I can tell, no," Peyton responded. "This is more about someone being really interested in history. They want the figurines for a private collection and are willing to pay a hundred thousand for their retrieval. The figurines are pretty small, so it's not like they would be worth that much even if they were melted down, and they couldn't identify them other than to mention they represent Oriceran races."

Shay nibbled her lip. Even without taking a supersonic flight, she could set off in the morning, easily get to Oregon, do the job, and get back before dinner time.

Peyton was right. A mere six-figure payday generally wasn't usually worth it anymore, but sometimes you just picked up the quarter on the sidewalk in front of you.

"Any legends associated with the caves? Hostile frog guys? Giant spiders that eat people? Ghosts? Cave-protecting death cults?

Peyton laughed. "Nope, nothing credible. The main thing is getting to the location. Requires some cave diving, and you have to know exactly where you're going."

"And the client happens to know exactly where I need to go?"

"Yeah, because they sent someone in before. They drowned, but they managed to get off a little emergency drone transponder."

Shay snickered. "At least they're honest about the danger. Okay, tell the client I'll take the job. Just have to drop off Lily and Alison at Warehouse Two, then I'll go gear up at Warehouse Three."

"Lily and Alison together?" Peyton groaned.

"What? Do you suddenly have a problem with them?"

"No, it's just that I don't know if I can survive two teenage girls."

17

The good news was Shay hadn't run into any frogmen, death cultists, or giant spiders. The bad news was the earthy and humid stench that clung to everything inside the cave filled her nostrils and made her want to gag.

The tomb raider continued wading through stagnant water filled with algae, insects, and who knew what disgusting parasites. She'd been in many caves in her short career as a tomb raider, and they never got any less annoying.

She slapped at the water. "Why can't I go after pirate treasure buried on a tropical island?"

The glamorous life of a tomb raider. Look at me, I'm wading through nature's sewage pipe. The area's arid, but this cave isn't. Nice how that shit works out. It's like a big joke at my expense.

Her diving equipment hung heavy on her back. From what the client had told Peyton, it'd be a good thirty minutes of walking before she hit the actual point of diving. She'd been walking almost that long. She couldn't verify anything with her assistant, though, since her communications had died once she was five minutes into the cave.

Something brushed against her leg.

Shay frowned. She had a needle gun hanging from her belt in case she needed to deliver a little underwater death, but taking on some monster in dark cave water struck her as high on the list of bad ideas. She just needed to find the damned figurines and get the hell out of there before some mud octopus ate her.

Gold. Everyone likes gold. Even early humans liked the shiny metal. What the hell is it about gold?

The splashes of water echoed as she made her way deeper into the tightening cave system.

Her headlamp and wrist light illuminated the rippling water and moist cave walls covered with fungus, moss, and algae. Life always found a way. A disgusting way, but still a way.

The flow of the water picked up as she approached a deep opening. She could hear the sound of rushing water below.

Almost there. Time to gear up, I guess.

Shay lowered her mask and connected her tanks and oxygen lines. She took a moment to equalize the pressure in her system before grabbing a coiled nylon line off her belt. The tomb raider found an outcropping to tie the line off to before using it to slowly climb into the dark rushing water below.

She hissed as the current caught her leg. Her heart sped up, but she took a few deep breaths and kept moving down. She wouldn't be swept away as long as she held onto the line, and even if she were, she had oxygen.

I can swim against the current. It wouldn't be fun, but I could do it.

Shay took a few deep breaths.

Good thing I'm not afraid of dark spaces or water.

An image invaded her mind, tumbling logs in a deadly maze. She winced.

Sure, she'd almost been buried alive on her first real tomb raid, but she'd gotten her revenge on the lake later with the help of Daniel Goldstein sponsoring a return to the lake.

Is that what I need? A bunch of CIA money and a full team? Screw that. I've done tons of underwater raids since then. This isn't such a bad deal, and the past doesn't predict the future. I can do this.

Shay continued her descent, the current weakening as she moved deeper into the dark, watery abyss. She had plenty of air left, and not a single hostile monster, animal, or human had come anywhere near her, unless she was counting the giardia in the water.

She was feeling pretty relaxed, even bored, when she saw a hand.

Shay kept hold of her nylon line with her left hand and raised her needle gun with her right, her heart pounding.

Well, at least I'm not gonna die in my kitchen.

The tomb raider aimed the weapon but didn't fire. The gloved hand was waving. No. Not waving—it was moving with the slow underwater current.

She shifted her head to illuminate the rest of her new friend. A half-rotted corpse stared back at her.

Shay took a deep breath, trying to keep the bile down. She hooked the needle gun back onto her belt and took in the disturbing sight.

Fuck. Guess I found the poor bastard who tried to find the figurines before me.

The man's legs had been pinned by rock and mud against the cave wall, and the rips in his gloves suggested he'd spent his last few moments desperately clawing at the rocks to try to free himself.

Good news is, I know I'm in the right spot.

Shay did her best to ignore the half-decayed water-logged corpse just yards away from her as she carefully searched the area for any hint of the figurines. With only her two lights available, she decided on a systematic approach. She started a few yards above the body, and inch by inch moved her head and hand to illuminate a new stretch of wall.

The seconds ticked along until they were minutes. Plenty of rocks, but nothing shiny.

Wonder how the client knew it was here? Did they do an aquatic drone survey first?

Shay snickered, thinking that might have been a good idea. Going to Lake Toplitz the second time with a team and being more deliberate with her exploration hadn't been the worst thing in the world. Not every tomb raid might lend itself to that sort of strategy, but she'd fallen into a pattern of trying to get in and out at maximum speed.

It did help reduce her run-ins with assholes like Yulia, but whether she was killed by an ice spear or crushed by logs, she would be just as dead in the end.

Something shone in the beam of her wrist light.

What do we have here?

Shay glanced between the shining material and the body. A few yards. He'd almost found the treasure but then ended up dead in some cave in Oregon.

Was it a good or a bad way to die? She didn't know, but she'd prefer not to die either in her kitchen from a gunshot wound or from running out of oxygen in a cave anytime soon.

Dying's easy. Living's the hard part.

She let go of the line and swam toward the source of the shine. Closer to it now, she could identify the mud-encrusted arm of a small figurine.

Okay, that's one. Good start.

The tomb raider carefully dug a small golden figurine out of the mud and rock. She did her best to wipe off some of the grime, but her thick gloves and the conditions made it difficult.

The small golden figurine was crude in design, but identifiably humanoid with pointed ears. Any doubts Shay'd had about it being merely stylized were erased by the crude etchings on the body. She couldn't read the words, but she recognized some of the shapes. It wasn't elf script, but rather Gnomic from what she could tell. She deposited the figurine in a mesh bag clipped to her belt.

Gnomes sure get around. Or maybe this is just the Oriceran equivalent of a copyright notice.

The next agonizing ten minutes passed as she carefully scraped and pulled around the area. She was just about to give up when she found the corner of another figurine. It was larger, and maybe it was just her recent trip to the

Great Treaty, but she thought it looked a lot like a Kilomea. Again, something resembling Gnomic script was written on it.

I need to wrap this up sooner than later. Don't want to be hanging out down here and worried about reserve oxygen.

Shay continued her excavation near the previous finds. It took fifteen minutes of careful work before she found the edge of the last figurine. She lost a few more minutes of oxygen freeing it: a thin humanoid with four arms.

Jackpot.

A satisfying smugness settled over the tomb raider as she slipped the figurine into her bag. When she looked up, her heart nearly stopped. Huge cracks had spread from her digging site.

Shit. Need to get out of here.

The wall collapsed, sending a wave of mud and rock straight toward Shay. She kicked her legs to send herself back toward her safety line, but debris pinned her against the cave wall, much like the poor corpse of the other tomb raider. The latest cave shift sent his body tumbling into the darkness below.

Shay stretched reaching toward the white line in the dark water.

Just a few more inches, damn it.

Even though most of the rock and dirt had continued into the depths, if she couldn't get to the line she didn't think she'd be able to pull herself out of the rock and mud holding her in place. The cave would gain a new body for the next tomb raider to gawk at.

Come on, come on. I can do this.

Shay's fingers reached the line, and then she got her

hand around it. She tugged and managed a firm grasp with both hands.

Three…two…one.

With a push and a yank at the same time, her foot wrenched free, and she immediately started swimming back up. She didn't look down until she was only waist deep in the stagnant water of the upper cave.

Shay pulled her mask off and bent over, taking deep breaths. She'd been deep underground by herself with not even Peyton on comm. If she hadn't been able to free herself, she would have been dead in less than an hour, once her air ran out.

Shit, that was too damned close.

She straightened up and shook her head. It was always too damned close, whether it was an army of cursed invisible swordsmen, frogmen, French retrieval specialists, or possessed elves with alien stones.

The tomb raider burst out laughing. Her life was insane, and the only thing she could do was enjoy every minute of it.

1 8

———

Shay settled into a loveseat in her living room, stifling a slight yawn. It was just as she'd predicted. She'd been able to do the entire job including the delivery in a single day. It wasn't huge money by her standards, but the job, other than running into the corpse, had been almost an errand more than a tomb raid.

Yeah, I can say that because I didn't drown. Then again, if I had, I would have been dead.

With James in Las Vegas checking on some Brownstone Agency business with the local police, it left her with an open evening.

Alison was at her house, spending the night chatting with some of her friends from school. Shay half-suspected she was talking to a boy, but she figured if she didn't ask then she wouldn't have to lie to the paranoid James about it.

His daughter is growing more beautiful by the day. He's just gonna have to learn to deal with that. Plus, Alison knows magic. She can handle herself.

That left Shay alone in her home with no pressing tomb raid or research she needed to worry about. She was still curious about why the Demon Generals' temporary leader might have been interested in the Anzick site, but the department head was still spooked by the whole experience. During their last phone call on the matter, he had been content to leave his old research alone for at least a few weeks.

Huh. It's been a while since I've had the chance to just sit and relax, unwind, and read. I should have brought some Anzick book to read. Maybe I would have stumbled onto something useful.

Shay smiled to herself as she lifted the book she'd brought instead from Warehouse Four. *The New Odyssey: A Modern Revised History Look at the Classic Myths.*

When was a god not a god? When they might have been an Oriceran. Sometimes Shay wondered how long it'd take for humanity to truly process what their false history had meant and how almost every major myth and legend at the heart of civilization had been influenced by Oricerans who had known exactly what they were doing.

Considering that the ancient beliefs were even baked into things like the days of the week, it was surprising how little resentment the average human felt toward Oricerans. Most people seemed more concerned about Oricerans coming to Earth and taking their jobs than what they might have done in the past.

We're a petty species. I'm still sure that shit will cause some major trouble in the future, but for now, everyone's too busy worrying about surviving.

Shay found herself detached from the whole idea. On a

certain level, she could understand why it was annoying that the Oricerans had manipulated human history, but on the other hand, humans had also participated in the deception. If anything, it felt like she should be angrier at the humans in the know than the Oricerans.

In addition, she'd lived her life in solitude, with only a recent expansion into having people near and dear to her. It was hard to get too worked up about what someone might have done to her ancestors thousands of years ago. No one could change the past, not even the most powerful wizard.

I can't change the world or the past. All I can do is find out the truth for myself and protect the people I care about. For now, that's the new life plan, and that's all I care about. I'm sure we'll find out in a thousand years that all Oriceran history is a lie made up by some other strange planet. Maybe James'.

Shay snickered at the thought. After a moment, she opened her book and read the first passage aloud.

"Long, torturous thought and deliberation have gone into decoding the myths and legends that formed the basis of the Ancient Greek world. Long thought to be fanciful exaggerations or mere just-so stories, the existence of Oriceran has forced many classical scholars to go back and ask themselves, 'What if everything the ancients said were true?'"

Shay smiled to herself.

What if?

Something wasn't right.

Shay shot out of bed, alert. Her heart was racing. Whatever else might have changed, her decade-long career as a professional killer had left her permanently a light sleeper. The smallest irregularity at night led to her waking up. The big exception was when James was there. Sleeping in his arms, even the jaded Shay felt safe.

Of course, it was a double-edged sword.

Wish James didn't snore so loudly.

She frowned and shook her head. James wasn't there. He was in Las Vegas. So why had she woken up?

A couple more seconds passed before she realized her cell phone was ringing.

"Who the fuck is calling me at 4:30 in the morning?"

The tomb raider snatched the phone from the nightstand and frowned.

"Peyton? Why the hell is he calling?"

Her heart kicked into overdrive. Peyton wasn't brave enough to piss her off with a pointless call, let alone a prank, which meant something very damned important was happening, such as a warehouse breach. His monitoring systems were supposed to send alerts to her phone as well as his, but the eager man was constantly tinkering with them so she couldn't be sure they were even working.

Shay accepted the call. "What's going on, and how much shooting or stabbing will it involve?"

Peyton let out a long yawn. "Not sure yet, but probably some shooting and a little stabbing."

"Huh? What do you mean? Why the fuck did you call and wake my ass up?"

"Because the Professor contacted me and woke *my* ass up." He sighed. "I liked it better when he contacted you directly and left me out of the loop. Now he calls me first half the time, and it's weird talking to a guy who calls me 'lad' and says 'aye.'"

"Well, you're my assistant, and I might not have access to my phone, but I'm still confused." Shay rubbed her tired eyes. "What did the professor have to say?"

"The Professor has a job for you. Expiration date of today. If you don't call and arrange to meet with him within an hour, he's moving on to someone else, and he'll be, and I quote, 'Very disappointed in Miz Carson.'"

Shay shot out of bed. "What the fuck? A job, and I have to meet with him in an hour?"

"That's what he said. He also said don't bother calling him, just show up at the Leanan Sídhe in an hour."

"Okay, okay. I'm up. I'm up." Shay shook her head. "This better damn well be important."

Shay frowned as she approached the front door of the Leanan Sídhe. The pub wasn't going to be open for several hours, but she assumed the man hadn't been totally drunk when he'd called Peyton and had directed her to come there.

What the fuck is so important that the Professor is snapping his fingers to get me here?

She looked up and down the sparse post-dawn streets before approaching the front door and trying it. It was open.

Her hand slipped inside her jacket. Maybe the whole damned thing was a trap.

Shay frowned and stepped inside. No one else was inside the bar except two men in the back: the Professor and Correk.

It was a trap, all right.

She narrowed her eyes and marched over to their table. "What's *he* doing here? If this is about the damned egg, I'm not fucking giving it up, so waking me up at the ass-crack of dawn was a waste of everyone's time."

She dropped her hands to her sides. She was pissed at Correk, but she didn't plan on shooting him. Not yet, anyway.

The Professor smirked. There were no empty glasses in front of him and no rosiness to his cheeks. Apparently, he had a limit to when he'd start drinking.

Correk raised his hand. "This isn't about the egg. I come in peace. There's no argument between the two of us. I came to offer help, and you'd be wise to accept it given what you're about to do."

Shay frowned and looked at the two men. She doubted they'd pull some long-play scheme just for the egg, and the Professor had seemed fine with her keeping the melting artifact of doom.

The tomb raider sat down reluctantly, her face twitching. "Help with what? What's the Professor got for me?"

"Anzick. I know that the Demon Generals were seeking information on the site from your department head at UCLA."

"How the hell do you know about that?" She rolled her eyes and waved a hand. "Don't answer it. It probably ends with, 'I'm the Fixer. Of course, I know.' Well, Fixer, it doesn't matter. The Demon Generals who were interested in the site only cared because of a new leader. I took care of that gentleman in a rather permanent way. Those bastards will stop caring about ancient history to artifacts soon enough, so it doesn't matter if they got the coordinates from the old papers."

"Coordinates. That makes sense." Correk nodded slowly. "It's a good thing more competent people haven't come looking for that information."

"I told you, I ended it. Those assholes aren't gonna be artifact-hunting anymore."

The Professor leaned back in his seat, observing them in silence.

The Fixer sighed. "Unfortunately, you taking care of their leader isn't enough. I wish it were that simple. Unfortunately, the gang was even more short-sighted than you realize."

Shay frowned. "What do you mean?"

"They were blabbering too much, trying to look like big men among their fellow criminals. Their new leader should have taught them the value of discretion."

The tomb raider shook her head. "What am I missing?"

"My wife, Leira, is a bounty hunter." A proud smile crossed the Light Elf's face. "The original of the modern sort, really. James Brownstone is simply following in her footsteps." He shrugged. "But anyway, an informant of hers recently coughed up some information to save himself."

The tomb raider smirked. "Apparently, your wife rolls a lot like James."

"She can be very persuasive and stubborn when she needs to be. She also shares his penchant for destroying Japanese gangster organizations."

Shay nodded. "Definitely like James. So what did this informant say?"

Correk frowned. "That the Montana burial site is on the lips of a lot of seriously dangerous people in the dark underworld."

"Why exactly? Dr. Weber says he thought it used to be a portal to Oriceran. Why would they care so much about that? It's not the only site like that. If he'd proved that thirty years ago it might have been a big deal, but now it's just more proof of something we already know."

The Fixer nodded. "You're right. It isn't unique for that, but there are a lot of rumors that there's a powerful and extremely old artifact buried there. Some people claim the magic of ancient Oriceran kings is contained in it. Others claim it's a concentration of Rhazdon's dark magic."

Shay winced. Rhazdon was like Hitler, if he had been an Atlantean and controlled particularly powerful magic.

Correk leaned forward. "Others say it's something else entirely, perhaps some source of magic ancient and complicated even by the standards of Oriceran."

"Don't you know what it is?"

"Being the Fixer means I have access to certain spells and books. It doesn't make me omniscient." He shrugged. "The point is, I think you should go after this artifact immediately and expect the unexpected. Watch your back. This isn't going to be a simple artifact hunt, no matter what it looks like on the surface. I know that much."

Shay eyed the elf. "If it's so dangerous and important, why aren't *you* going?"

"I've got limitations due to my situation, and some recent encounters would make it dangerous for me to go there. I'd rather not upset the status quo too much in such a volatile situation."

The Professor cleared his throat. "Thirty million if you return the artifact, Miz Carson. You'll need to depart today, and unlike the egg, this time we can't let you keep it no matter what happens. Understood?"

Shay stared at the Professor. He wasn't wearing his customary amused smile or smirk. Even Smite-Williams could be serious when needed. The lack of booze probably helped.

She took a deep breath. "Fine, you've got yourself a tomb raider."

Someday, I'll spend weeks planning a raid and take my time. Always in such a damned hurry.

Ten minutes later, Shay was on the road again, dialing Peyton.

"Is this revenge for earlier?" he whined. "I'm sorry I woke you up, but the Professor made it clear the time limit was non-negotiable."

Shay snorted. "This isn't about revenge. It's about money. "The Professor offered me a thirty-million-dollar job. Correk was there to give me extra info on it."

"Thirty million?" Peyton fell silent for several seconds. "More melting eggs?"

"Even Correk doesn't seem to know what's up exactly, but it turns out I need to get to the Anzick site today before assholes show up and steal whatever it is. Probably some melt-the-whole-world kind of thing. Who the hell knows?"

Peyton laughed. "You'll probably get there and find out it was some dwarf's childhood sled."

Shay chuckled. "We can hope. Anyway, I need to get more background information on this, and we don't have a lot of time. I need you to arrange the transportation for Lily and me in the afternoon, then go prep our equipment. We're hitting this thing today. If those guys woke your ass up and my ass up this early, this isn't the kind of thing I can sleep on."

"Does Lily even know she's going? Plus, does she want to? I know we helped her, but that doesn't really change the whole watching-a-guy-get-melted-by-an-artifact thing. Maybe she's done with tomb raiding."

Can't blame her if she is. Not everyone has the stomach for every job.

Shay sighed. "I'll call her in a second. Can you do every-thing else for me?"

Peyton yawned. "Yeah, yeah. Aye, aye, ma'am. Better get started. Talk to you later." He disconnected.

Shay immediately dialed Lily.

The phone rang four times before the teen answered with a long yawn.

"Why are you calling me so early?"

"Major job. I want you to come, but I also understand if after what happened on the last job you don't want to."

Lily sighed. "Shay, if you need me, I'll be there. It's like you said the other night. If I want to walk this path, I'm going to have to get used to seeing freaky and disturbing stuff."

"If it makes you feel any better, I think we might be helping save the world this time. At least a little bit."

The teen chuckled. "And how much does that run these days? Helping to save the world?"

"Thirty million."

"It's hard to say no to helping save the world, especially when I'm getting a cut of thirty million."

Shay laughed. "See you later. I've got a few things to take care of before we head out."

A couple of hours later, Shay found her way to Prophecy Affiliates. It was surprisingly easy to find Tubal-Cain's business this time. She wondered if it helped that the mall had just opened, and the crowds weren't as thick.

Madge sat in her tiny chair, flipping through a tiny magazine. It was as ridiculous as it was cute.

She looked up, lowering her head and staring at Shay over the tops of her cat-eye glasses. "You're early."

"I need to talk to Tubal-Cain."

Madge shrugged and set her magazine down. "He's napping."

"Napping?"

The pixie laughed. "Did you think he never slept?"

"Maybe." Shay shrugged.

The pixie's wings fluttered, and she rose into the air. Shay watched, fascinated, as Madge lifted her round body with her tiny wings to fly between the desk and a nearby cabinet. She wasn't sure if the cabinet had been there before or if she just hadn't noticed it.

"If you're just here for gossip," the pixie commented, "I'm a better resource anyway. That gnome is in love with pointless riddles and vague phrasing."

"One second." Shay pointed toward the cabinet. "You still use filing cabinets?"

Madge nodded. "Yeah, to store my lunch."

She lifted her hand, and a shimmering wave came out and flowed toward the cabinet. It slid open. She peered inside at several tiny trays filled with what appeared to Shay to be colorful pellets, but she didn't want to embarrass herself by asking what pixies actually ate.

Madge waved her hand again, and the shimmering wave traveled again to the cabinet, and it closed itself. "Tubal-Cain's kind of a hoarder. Hates to get rid of anything." She grinned. "Besides, these were once owned by Eisenhower and spent some time in Area 51."

Shay resisted the urge to ask the pixie about Project Ragnarok or Project Nephilim. She had more pressing concerns.

"So there's a site in Montana, Anzick. Native site, big archaeology deal. Very important." The tomb raider shrugged. "I'm gonna cut to the chase. A guy I sort of work for has done a lot of research on this site, and he's found some evidence that it might have been the location of an ancient Oriceran portal. I didn't care that much before some criminals tried to steal his information about the site, and then the Fixer came and gave me a big speech about a dangerous artifact maybe being there."

Madge grimaced. "The Fixer? Ugh. He's got a few too many wands up his butt if you know what I mean."

Shay snickered. "Not gonna argue. He's alright, but we don't always see eye to eye."

"That's what having too much responsibility does for you, you know? That, and gives you wrinkles." She fluttered back over to her chair. "But Tightbutt Elf might be onto something this time."

"What do you mean?"

Madge shrugged. "There are a lot of stories that have been passed down among pixies for generations, and I mean pixie generations, not your sad little human years. I've heard some versions of this story that involve the place you mentioned."

Shay furrowed her brow. "What kind of stories?"

"Other species roaming this world." She gestured around. "Earth."

"So? We know that now. The Oricerans came here, and some stayed. Some didn't. They did a lot of stuff, like inspire religions. That's not news."

Madge let out a long, labored sigh and stared at Shay like she was an idiot. "I'm a pixie, honey. We wouldn't pass down a bunch of stories about other Oricerans wandering the Earth. We wouldn't find that strange. Keep up."

Shay shrugged. "Sorry. Go on."

Madge leaned forward, suddenly looking surprisingly sinister for something so small with such delicate wings. "These stories have been around for thousands of years about how you got other species coming here a lot more often than you'd like. Not Oricerans, but from other planets.."

"Shouldn't Oricerans be stopping that sort of thing?"

"Why? They aren't the planet's cops, and if these other

species weren't using magic that Oricerans could even understand, a lot of them would be just as clueless about these guys coming."

Shay stared at the pixie, frowning. Project Ragnarok. Project Nephilim. The government knew, and at least some of the Oricerans knew.

Maybe Dr. Weber had stumbled onto a far more important truth than anyone realized.

"Thanks, Madge. That's interesting, and maybe even a little helpful."

The pixie winked. "Keep your head on a swivel out there, honey. This world has a lot more to teach you, some of it deadly. I'll tell Tubal-Cain you stopped by when he wakes up."

Shay pulled the SUV off the dirt road. A short wooden fence surrounded the Anzick site. The simple structure was too low to do a good job of stopping people, so she presumed it was there to stop wandering animals. The actual dig site was a series of deep rectangular pits. A few no-trespassing signs were up, even though there hadn't been much active digging in years.

Unless Dr. Weber gets his way.

"Are we going to have to beat up some deputies?" Lily asked, pointing to one of the signs.

Shay shook her head. "Officially, I'm here as part of a preliminary survey for a new excavation with my department head's blessing and everything." She frowned. "That is gonna get annoying in the future."

"Why?"

"Because unlike tomb raiding, actual archaeology is very slow and methodical, and now Dr. Weber's expecting me to actually commit to an excavation." Shay shrugged. "I'll just have to make something up. As it is, I'm gonna have to lie about this. Besides, I don't have weeks to take off to sit in Montana. I'll be a real archaeologist in the future after I retire from tomb raiding."

Lily peered at the fences and the pits. "This isn't what I was expecting, to be honest."

Shay shrugged. "It's not some grand tomb. It's just where they found some bones and artifacts under what was likely a collapsed rock shelter. It's about as impressive as some of the other jobs I've taken you on."

"Those weren't just literally holes in the ground. I'm surprised anyone still cares about this place. Wouldn't they have found everything important already?"

Shay chuckled and opened the door and stepped out. "In the last few decades, they've come back with newer technology, and they discovered more bones and artifacts." She pointed to a pit in the corner. "That's the one place they found evidence of a more extensive structure a few years back. They didn't bother to follow up because of funding, but that's unfortunate because that's where things get interesting."

Lily exited the vehicle, and both tomb raiders went to the back. Shay opened the hatch to pull out a drone.

"What do you mean by interesting?" the teen asked.

"Subsequent excavation uncovered several out-of-place artifacts. They found several crystals that aren't indigenous to the area and have evidence of being artificially shaped by technologies far beyond not only the one in this area but any human culture at the time." Shay flipped a few switches on the drone and set it a few yards from the vehicle. "Make sure nobody ambushes us, Peyton."

"Will do," he responded in her earpiece. His voice was muffled, and she could hear chewing a second later.

Guess that explains why he's been so quiet. Kind of a blessing.

The drone hummed and whirred into the sky until it was hundreds of feet up.

Lily patted her tactical harness. Shay smiled. The girl was already internalizing good tactical awareness both pre- and post-battle. If her precognition couldn't save her, that very well might.

"So what about the crystals?" the girl asked. "They are all weird and artificial. They probably took them and did a bunch of tests, right?"

Shay grabbed a shovel from the back and tossed it to Lily, and picked up her own. "From what Dr. Weber said, all the crystals were stolen not that long after the last excavation. The archaeology community still doesn't want to admit this place might have anything to do with magic, and more than a few people have tried to argue the crystals never existed. That it was all a fraud by pro-Oriceran scholars." She headed toward the fence, Lily trailing after her.

"But you think the crystals were magical?"

Shay nodded. "Yeah." She frowned. "The only weird thing is that they've done preliminary magical surveys in the area. They've found traces of what might be magical energy, but not what they'd expect. I don't know all the details of why, but from what I've read, it's basically the wrong 'flavor.'"

If that pixie's right, then I think I know why. That might also be why no one serious has looked into this place.

Lily shrugged. "Maybe it's just like the magical version of finding some rusty old screw from centuries ago. Might not be a big deal. Some local rednecks probably stole the crystals to sell for dust."

Shay chuckled. "Could be. Again, I don't know the details, but those crystals probably had something to do with the portal if there was one here." She walked toward the fence. "We have the exact coordinates from Dr. Weber's old paper, so we're gonna do a little quick digging." She jumped to the top of the fence and then over.

Lily vaulted the fence using her free hand. "I don't get why no one else has done this. I mean, I know you said they lost funding, but this place has been here a long time, and no one has finished digging it up just because of one batch of stolen crystals?"

"Lots of controversy over the site for a lot of reasons. Some of it because it involved Native Americans, some of it because this is private land that's changed hands. After Weber's theories started spreading, a lot of reputable archaeologists didn't want to do more work, worrying about being associated with fringe pseudoarcheology. Like I said, even today, it's still got a little taint because of it. You have to understand, kid, that a lot of these archaeologists spent their entire careers saying people like Weber were idiots. Some of them are trying to run down the clock rather than admit they were wrong."

Lily laughed. "So the guys who are supposed to be figuring out the truth are ignoring it because they don't want to admit they were wrong?"

Shay grinned. "Funny how that works, isn't it?" She continued strolling to a pit at the other edge of the fenced area and slowed as she approached the edge, a frown build-ing. She dropped her shovel.

There was freshly disturbed soil near the pit, along with a huge hole in the center of the pile of dirt. From the even spread of the dirt, it looked as if someone had brought a massive drill and dug into the ground beside the existing pit.

The tomb raider hurried over to the hole and pulled out her phone to verify her coordinates. "Shit."

The new hole extended several yards, and there was a puddle of water at the bottom of it.

Lily jogged over. "I'm guessing that was where we were supposed to dig?" She sighed.

Shay's face tightened. "Someone got here first."

The teen's eyes widened, and she jerked her head around. "Something's coming."

Peyton cleared his throat. It took the tomb raider a few seconds to realize it was him and not Lily.

"There's a problem," he declared.

"Problem?"

Shay unholstered her gun. "Besides the fact that someone beat us to the super-deadly artifact?"

Lily dropped her shovel and pulled out her gun as well.

"All my cameras are frosting over on the drone," Peyton explained.

She looked up. The black dot floated high in the sky, nowhere near high enough that temperature should be such an issue, especially in Montana during the summer.

"Crap," Peyton shouted. "The drone just stopped trans-mitting."

A few seconds passed before Shay realized the drone

was falling from the sky, something glinting around it. It smashed into the ground in the distance with a surprisingly loud crash given its small size.

"Peyton?" Shay crouched low, her gun ready. She looked back and forth for an enemy. "Peyton?"

Nothing but static.

Lily swallowed. "That was definitely magic. I'm not getting any visions, but I can sense the magic."

A loud pop ripped through the air, and the two women spun toward the source. Something was zooming right toward them: a semi-translucent blue sphere.

Shay pushed Lily into a pit and threw herself in right after. The sphere smashed right where they'd been standing, shattering into hundreds of pieces. The tomb raider covered Lily's body with hers. Several pieces of debris slammed into her, a few ripping through her shirt and back and burning.

Shit. This hurts, but wait…it's not too hot. It's too cold. Oh fuck.

The tomb raider gritted her teeth at the pain and hopped back to her feet as she spun toward the site of impact. Lily stood and shook her head.

Yulia Solokova stood there, clad all in white, her wand in hand, a dozen small blue stones orbiting her and her wand at the ready. "Convenient that you're both here. Convenient indeed. I don't believe in luck, but this might change my mind."

There are a lot more of those blue stones than I've seen her have before. What does that mean? She's more powerful now? And what the hell? Was she in that ball of ice?

Shay glared at Yulia. "This isn't Antarctica. It's Montana in the summer. You're at a disadvantage here, bitch."

At a minimum, Shay hoped the witch couldn't pull off summoning ice hands and walls as easily.

"Keep telling yourself that, Aletheia." Yulia shot Lily a cold smile. "You have something that belongs to me, little Gray Elf."

Lily lifted her gun. "For my father, bitch." She opened fire. The bullet dropped to the ground inches in front of the witch, encased in ice. The girl kept pulling the trigger until the gun clicked empty, but none of the bullets made it through. It took several clicks before she stopped. She ejected the magazine and reloaded but didn't fire again.

The Ice Witch watched with an amused smirk. "I allowed you two to live in Antarctica so you would have time to reflect on your defeat and know fear." She grinned. "There's been enough time."

Shay hopped out of the pit opposite the witch. "Come on, Lily."

The girl narrowed her gray eyes on Yulia and jumped out of the pit. "You're not leaving here alive, bitch. I don't care what it takes."

Yulia shook her head, chuckling. The blonde patted a pocket in her white leather jacket. "I just came here for the artifact, but killing you both will be such a wonderful bonus." She whipped up her wand and disturbingly familiar blue hexagonal patterns formed in the front.

Here it comes.

Shay and Lily jumped out of the way when sharp ice lances emerged and flew toward them. The pair ran toward the SUV.

The tomb raider blasted a few quick shots off at Yulia but didn't do any better than her protégé at hurting her. "You've wounded her before, Lily, which means the damned shield is at least partially about concentration or angle or some shit."

Lily ducked as an ice lance flew right over her, her expression dark. "I don't just want to wound her. I want to kill her."

Shay grabbed a frag grenade from her belt and pulled the pin. She waited before throwing it. The grenade exploded a couple yards away from the witch. There was a bright blue flash, and dozens of pieces of icy shrapnel fell to the ground, but Yulia didn't even look to have been scratched.

Need a better strategy, and fast.

The wounds in Shay's back continued to throb, but she ignored them.

The tomb raider's major advantage this time was that she hadn't decided to fight an Ice Witch in the middle of Antarctica. The dry environment and summer conditions should be enough to somewhat even the playing field. She just needed a weapon that could pierce the woman's defenses.

Shay's eyes widened, and her gaze shot to the still-open SUV. "Lily, I'm gonna make a break for the *Masamune*. That should be able to cut through her—"

Agony shot through the tomb raider's shoulder, and she tumbled to the ground. The ultimate oxymoron: burning cold. A sharp shard of crystal-blue ice was embedded in her left shoulder.

Lily threw a couple of grenades at Yulia and hurried

over to Shay to help her up. The pair stumbled toward the SUV.

The tomb raider gritted her teeth. Her left arm was useless now.

This shit is going from bad to worse. Just need thirty seconds for a potion.

Yulia chanted something in Russian and swirled her wand. The blue glyphs hanging in the air brightened, and a solid, smooth sphere of ice started growing in front of her.

Each step jolted Shay's wounds, spreading the pain farther. They arrived at the SUV just as the Russian stopped chanting. The now-massive sphere hurtled toward them.

Shay and Lily leaped over the hood of the SUV. The sphere slammed into the vehicle and knocked it onto its side. Lily's reflexes allowed her to roll out of the way just in time, but the wounded Shay took a direct smash on her legs. She cried out in pain. Something crunched, and pure fire shot up her leg.

Fuck that hurts, but at least we've got some cover for a few seconds. Got to keep it together. We can still win this.

With a shaking hand, she yanked the shard out of her shoulder. She screamed and tossed the blood-covered ice to the ground. She pulled one of her two healing potions out of a belt pouch and downed it.

"Aletheia," Yulia called. "It's so delicious that I can finally pay you back for what you did to me on that island, but I want you to know this doesn't end here. Your death is just the beginning of your humiliation."

You want me to beg for my life, bitch? Not gonna happen.

"What do we do, Shay?" Lily whispered.

Shay took a deep breath and slowly let it out as her wounds sealed and the pain vanished. "Attack her from both sides. Just need to distract her enough."

Yulia chuckled. "Or did I already kill you with that last attack? That would be disappointing. I know a lot about you, Aletheia. More than you realize. I'll kill that little bitch you have with you, but even that won't be the end, Shay Carson."

The tomb raider jerked her head up. "What are you talking about?"

"You think I don't know who you really are? My power's been growing. After I kill you and the girl, I think I'll travel to LA. Imagine what people would say when I kill your precious James Brownstone. I'll kill him and crucify him in ice. I'd love to see that on the news."

Shay gritted her teeth. "You stay away from him, bitch."

"No. I want you to die here, knowing that I'll destroy your lover as well. His death will be slow and agonizing, and he'll die cursing your name and ever knowing you."

Shay jumped up and unloaded several rounds, but none made it past the witch's defenses.

Yulia wagged her finger. "Did you actually think you could win against me? Pathetic. You just got lucky during our first encounter." She sneered and started chanting in Russian. More glyphs inlaid in encircled hexagonal patterns appeared in the air, and several ice balls started forming.

"Any visions?" Shay asked.

Lily ran a hand through her hair, her eyes wide. "Nothing. I'm sorry."

"Yulia was surprising me on jobs long before I met you."

Shay ejected her magazine and reloaded. "Just need to find the weak spot."

"But where?"

"If one of us can just get behind her, that might work." Shay peeked over the hood. Three massive ice spheres hung in front of the witch. "But we have to mo—"

Yulia stopped chanting, and the deadly ice hurtled toward them.

Fuck. At least it's not my kitchen or some damned cave underground.

A bright flash blinded Shay, and she blinked her eyes a few times until they adjusted. A small golden orb spun in front of the SUV, a pulsating kaleidoscopic forcefield extending from it on either side. Piles of broken ice lay on the ground beyond it.

Daniel Goldstein stood there on the side closer to her in a black suit and silver glasses, as she'd seen him on previous occasions, but this time he wore a strange glossy black harness over his shoulders and around his chest. "Hmm. That worked better than I thought it would." He pressed a button, and the harness unbuckled and dropped to the ground. "Like my rabbi back home used to always tell me, you just need to use the right tool for the right job." The CIA agent smiled. "And you don't always need magic when you have nice toys."

Lily blinked and poked her head up. "Who the heck is he?"

Shay chuckled. "Lily, this is Daniel Goldstein. He's CIA." She looked back at the man. "You tomb raiding on the side now, Goldstein?"

"Tomb raiding? No, but the fact you've just asked that

explains a lot about you, Professor Carson, and why you feel so free to tell your little friend about who I work for. I'll trust in your discretion in this manner, both of you." The man offered them a bright smile and turned back to the scowling Yulia. "Snegurka, huh? I've read so many reports about you, but now I meet you. It's sort of a sick honor. It's my lucky day."

The Russian witch narrowed her eyes. "If you value your life, you'll leave."

"Can't do that." Daniel shook his head. "I've got an investment in Professor Carson." He glanced her way. "Who I'm beginning to believe is a lot more than a simple archaeologist, and the fact that you're here only proves it."

Yulia snapped her wand up and blasted several more ice spears toward them. They slammed into the golden orb's shield and bounced back, falling to the ground. She hissed in anger.

Daniel reached into his jacket and pulled out an odd silver handgun. The barrel was too small for it to be a .22. He eyed Shay and Lily. "I can cover you if you want to leave."

Shay shook her head. "I owe that bitch." She nodded toward Lily. "And Yulia fucked over her father."

Lily gave an angry nod.

Yulia pointed her wand at the sky. She was now all but screaming in Russian. Floating glyphs painted the air around her, and her eyes started glowing azure. Blue flashes appeared in the sky.

Daniel aimed his gun at the witch. "Whatever she's doing, it's not good, but I don't think even this baby will be enough to get through her basic shield."

"I've got something that will." Shay holstered her gun, jogged to the back of the overturned SUV, and pulled out the Masamune *tachi*. She hurried back over to Lily and the CIA agent. "I just need her distracted. If I can get close with this, I can end all of this."

Daniel nodded. "Just be ready to go when I give the signal."

Lily frowned. "But what's the signal?"

"Oh, you'll know." He winked.

Dozens of encircled hexagonal patterns of light winked into existence in the sky around the trio. The stones that had floated around Yulia before now whirled around her so fast that they looked like twisting blue ropes.

Daniel snapped his fingers. The force field disappeared, and the golden orb dropped to the ground. Lily sprinted forward but not directly at Yulia. She opened fire.

The CIA agent pulled the trigger on his silver pistol. A thin needle shot out. When it reached the witch, it exploded. Blood dripped down cuts in her face, and she jerked her wand down.

Shay sprinted forward, raising her sword.

This shit is over, Yulia.

A deadly hail of dozens of ice lances blasted from the sky. Lily whirled and spun. The projectiles embedding themselves behind or in front of her.

Daniel slapped his watch. The frozen missiles bounced off an invisible forcefield mere inches from his body.

An explosion of pain shot through Shay's back and leg as three lances impaled her. She continued her charge, her sword raised high. Each step was excruciating, but she was so close now. So damned close.

Yulia glared at her and aimed her wand.

Too late, bitch.

With a scream, Shay pierced the witch's heart with her sword. She pushed forward until the blade stuck out the other side.

Yulia blinked and coughed up blood. Her wand dropped to the ground, along with the blue stones.

The tomb raider coughed up blood as well and managed a laugh before falling to the ground.

I win.

Yulia stumbled forward a few steps. "But I was to be immortal." She fell to the ground face-first and stopped breathing. Her crystal-blue eyes stared at Shay.

"Fuck," Shay moaned, rolling onto her side. She coughed up more blood. Each breath hurt.

Lily and Daniel rushed to her side.

The tomb raider looked up at Lily. "You okay, kid?"

The girl nodded quickly, tears streaming down her face. "Shay, you're dying."

She winced and forced herself onto her knees. "Wouldn't be the first time. Just…get these things out of me, and I can use a potion."

Daniel gave her a grim nod. "Hold her, Lily. Sorry, Professor Carson, this is going to hurt like hell."

"Just do it," Shay barked through gritted teeth.

The CIA agent leaned down and yanked out the first lance. He pulled out the second, and then with a mighty kick knocked out the third. Shay screamed each time.

She fell to the ground trying to reach the potion in her belt, but her hand wouldn't move.

Fuck. At least I took down that bitch. Sorry, James.

Lily ripped the potion out of her belt pouch. "Just stay with me, Shay." She uncorked the potion.

"Glad I could help you get revenge for your dad, Lily."

"Screw that, just stay with me." Lily poured the potion down her throat.

Shay smiled as the darkness took her.

Shay didn't awaken to a boring angeltopia or a fiery inferno. She blinked her eyes, trying to take in where she was. Soft leather seats, the back of a car. They were moving.

Someone was talking. Lily?

"Yes. She's okay. We're getting a ride back to the airport. Yeah. Yeah. No one blames you for not being able to stop weird magical interference. Talk to you later."

"Was that the Pizza King?" Shay asked. She was still unsure how much Daniel had figured out about her and didn't see any reason to give him free information. A CIA agent of all people could understand the need for code names.

Lily looked over her shoulder. "Oh, you're awake. Yeah, that was him. He was freaking."

"I'm not dead?"

Daniel chuckled from the driver's seat. "Not yet."

Shay shook her head. "Yulia?"

"Oh, now, *she's* dead. Very dead. Nice job, by the way. She's killed more than a few people who work for the Company."

"And what about the artifact?"

Daniel reached into his pocket and pulled out a small stone. Shay couldn't read it, but she recognized the style of the writing. It was extraterrestrial, the same kind as the other stones she'd either examined or had images of.

"It's not an artifact," the CIA agent explained. "At least not in the magical sense."

"You're not gonna let me keep that, are you?"

Daniel shook his head. "I will let you take pictures of it, though. Consider it a bonus for taking down Snegurka."

Shay snorted. "Pictures aren't worth thirty million dollars."

"You know what they say—money isn't everything." He grinned. "I do apologize, though."

"Nah, you saved our lives. That means something." Shay stared down at the alien stone. The Fixer had said the magical underworld was in an uproar, but why would any of them, let alone, Yulia, be obsessed with recovering an alien stone?

That evening after dropping off her gear at Warehouse Three, Shay headed immediately to Prophecy Affiliates, hoping they were still open. She could never tell, given they didn't post any business hours.

Madge acts like the gnome's so busy, but I never see anyone else here when I come.

The pixie sat in her little chair again reading a ridiculously tiny magazine. Shay wasn't sure if the size of the magazine or the fact that anyone still was reading paper magazines this far into the twenty-first century bothered her more.

Madge looked up at Shay entered. "You're not dead. Congratulations."

"Thanks. I try." Shay shrugged. "Is he here?"

"Maybe."

The tomb raider groaned. "Maybe? Look, it's been a really long day, and I almost died a couple of times, so… work with me, just a little."

Madge set her magazine down. "No, first I need a little fee."

"Fee?" Shay narrowed her eyes.

The pixie grinned. "Tell me if my joke is funny by human standards."

Shay shrugged. "Okay, whatever. Go for it."

Madge floated right in front of Shay with a serious look on her face. "What's the difference between a pregnant woman and a lightbulb?"

The tomb raider shrugged. "I don't know. What?"

"You can unscrew a lightbulb."

Shay chuckled despite the fact that a pixie was stalling her with dirty jokes. "That's halfway decent."

"Okay, one more." Madge held up a finger. "A husband and wife were talking at dinner. The husband asks the wife, 'How come you never tell me when you orgasm?' Do you know what the wife told him?"

"No. What?"

"I don't like calling you at work."

Shay snickered. "Okay, you've got a couple of decent jokes there, if you're planning to switch to stand-up comedy, but I really need to see the gnome now."

Madge gave Shay a predatory grin. Seeing it on such a small creature only made it more unnerving.

"Tell me a dirty joke, then. You don't need to know why I'm collecting them, but I am." She crossed her arms.

Shay rolled her eyes. "What the fuck? Have you been hanging around Smite-Williams?"

The tomb raider had called the Professor on her way to the mall to explain what had happened. He seemed more amused than annoyed. He wasn't willing to pay

Shay thirty million for an object the CIA now had, but he did pay her a few million for her services rendered. She'd at least kept the object out of the hands of an evil witch.

Ah, Miz Carson. Another alien stone? Interesting. It seems the secret is spreading farther than anyone would know. Soon, I suspect, it won't be so secret.

"Who is Smite-Williams?" Madge asked, bringing Shay back to her immediate situation.

"A dirty old man I know." She sighed and rubbed the back of her neck, trying to think of a good joke. "Okay, why don't witches wear underwear?"

Madge shrugged. "I don't know why."

"To get a better grip on their brooms."

The pixie shook her head. "I don't get it."

Shay smirked. "Trust me, it's funny. Now, can I see the gnome already?"

"Keep your shirt on." Madge fluttered over the door in the back and knocked.

Shay wondered if Tubal-Cain could even hear it.

The door opened a moment later, and the gnome yawned.

"Napping again?"

He shrugged. "My work is very tiring." He nodded to the room. "Let's talk about whatever has you in such a rush. Of course, humans are *always* in a rush."

Shay stepped inside the back room, which was far different than the last time she'd been in it, and not just because it was larger than the entire main room. A gnome-sized recliner sat in the corner of a maroon-carpeted room. A crystal chandelier floated in the center with no visible means of support. In addition, several gray settees lay scattered about the room.

Does he sit around with a bunch of gnomes drinking bourbon on weekends?

"I'm still working on your little seeing project, Miz Carson," the gnome explained. "And that isn't something you can hurry."

"That's not why I'm here. I need another favor. Well, not a favor. I'll pay or grab whatever you need to make this happen."

"I'll take a favor as a payment." The gnome looked Shay up and down. "And what is it that you need?"

"A way to protect someone I love in case, in this case someone I love who has a habit of ending up in dangerous situations."

An exasperated look spread over the gnome's face. "You're talking about James Brownstone?"

Shay nodded. Even though they'd won against Yulia with Daniel's help, the woman's threat still echoed in the tomb raider's mind.

James was great when he saw the enemy coming, but in the course of her tomb raiding, Shay had run into countless beings who might be able to surprise him. Could even the great James Brownstone deal with an invisible army if they went after him? A *Rusalka*? No, if her work might put him in danger, then it was her responsibility to make sure that he was safe.

Tubal-Cain snorted. "I really thought you were smarter than this."

"What the hell are you talking about? Smarter than what?"

"Love?" He clucked his tongue. "You've fallen for the most dangerous weapon on any world, love with a little hootchie-cootchie on the side. Maybe even the main dish." The gnome gave her a little nudge. "Seriously?"

Shay snorted. "I don't need lessons on how to be a better, smarter human from a gnome."

He smirked. "Wisdom is wisdom, regardless of species."

"I just need a way to keep him safe. He's got toys of his own, but I don't trust them, and they aren't automatic. He could get surprised tomorrow."

"There's no way to keep someone you love safe forever." Tubal-Cain hopped into his recliner with a smile and folded his hands on his lap.

Shay stood in front of the settee. "But there's a way to keep him safe?"

Tubal-Cain shrugged. "I mean, I have a few things that can put someone in amber or a deep sleep. I call that one 'the Sleeping Beauty.' That witch and her loom were no joke."

"How is that keeping them safe?"

"Well, it's not keeping them safe as much as preserving them, and that's my point. When you love someone, those kinds of ideas have to come off the table. Have to play nice. You want your loved one out in the world." He punctuated his rant by throwing his short arms as wide as he could manage. "And that complicates things."

A deep voice sounded from an unseen scratchy intercom. "You're in trouble, girl. Love fucks everything up," Madge offered. "Makes it all unpredictable."

Shay slapped her hands on her hips, frowning at Tubal-Cain and waiting for him to take her request seriously.

"Shall I start singing Andrew Lloyd Webber?" the gnome asked with a grin. "About love and it changing things?"

The tomb raider shot a glare at him. "If you can't give me something to make sure James is safe, then give me something to make sure I can really fuck with the other guy. Best defense is a good offense and all that."

Tubal-Cain chuckled. "Ah, well, now *that* I can do. Just remember all the warnings I've given you about magical artifacts?"

"If I turn into a bird saving James, big fucking deal."

"Very well, then. Follow me." He waved his arms. "Squint."

"Huh?"

"Squint." The gnome nodded toward a wall. "That way."

Shay turned her head and squinted, and a doorway appeared. She blinked.

"You're letting me into your inner sanctum?" She eyed the gnome, surprised at the risk he was taking.

Tubal-Cain let out a sharp laugh and shook his head. "Inner sanctum? Hardly. This is just the overflow. Don't get too excited." He moved to the door and opened it.

Shay stepped inside. Piles upon piles of boxes, bags, and sacks of every material and design filled the large chamber. The lounge she'd just been in appeared to be larger than the main shop, and this room was larger than both of them put together.

"Is this on Earth?" Shay asked.

The gnome snorted as he started burrowing through a pile of boxes. "Do you honestly expect me to answer that?"

The tomb raider shrugged. "It was worth a try."

Tubal-Cain started throwing boxes over his shoulder. "Where was it…or did I sell it to that annoying elf?" He pulled out a small black metal box. He shook it, and something light bounced against the thin walls. "Here we go." He nodded to himself, a satisfied look on his face.

Shay eyed the box. "What's in there?"

He walked over to Shay and raised the hinged lid. A large jeweled scarab was in the box.

"What was with the shaking? Weren't you worried about damaging it?"

"Oh, no. It's far more important to make sure it's in a resting state. It's a real bitch when it's not, and the box gets opened."

Shay eyed the scarab. "Wait, this isn't just an artifact, then?"

Tubal-Cain gave her a wide grin. "Oh, no. This isn't a beetle, but it's still very much alive, and very, very hungry. This little fellow can chew through pretty much anything, and I mean *anything*, including magical shields. It's also very, very tough. It was created here on Earth, in your ancient Egypt, with the aid of Atlantean magic." His smile disappeared. "A question remains whether it was supposed to be used as a tool for waste management or something far darker, but given how the Atlanteans were, I'd suspect the latter."

She nodded slowly. "Okay, so it's a super-beetle that can eat anything. How do I…control it?"

"I'll write down the incantation for you phonetically. I suspect you don't speak Old Egyptian."

"Nope. Somehow I missed that in school."

Tubal-Cain let out a dark chuckle. "It's easy otherwise.

Shake the box to make sure it's not active. If it is, you'll hear it in there scurrying about. If that's the case, you'll have to wait for at least a half-hour."

"So it can eat through anything but not that box?"

"Everything in the world has a weakness, but be aware that the box isn't that impressive. It can be easily damaged by anything other than the beetle." The gnome closed the lid and handed the box to her.

Shay shook the box but didn't hear any scurrying. "Okay, shake it. Wake it up with the incantation. Anything else?"

"You must see the target in your head as you use the incantation. This is where things get dangerous. You must be very specific and focused when invoking the scarab, or you'll send it after the wrong target. If you've done everything properly, it'll consume the target but nothing else."

She frowned. "And if I screw up?"

"Well, let's just say I recommend you only use this scarab once, and only when everything else has failed."

Shay stared at the box. "This sounds pretty dangerous. You sure you want to give it to me?"

"No, but I will." The gnome smiled, but it didn't reach his eyes. "Good luck, Miz Carson. I pray that you never need the scarab. And you owe me one large favor."

Shay smiled, her arm around James' waist as they stood near Peyton's oven in Warehouse Two. They had just gotten through the introductions, since this was the first time Lily and Brownstone had actually met. Now Lily and Alison leaned against a table, chatting.

"We've been talking about moving out of the tunnels," Lily explained. "Especially since I have a lot of money now. We'll maybe get some decent work set up for the rest of the tunnel kids; you know, like information broker stuff. They could work on that while I'm doing tomb raiding. Harry's already been trying to make it happen, but a little money and a permanent place to live would help, I think."

James chuckled. "Maybe Tyler could use some subcontractors."

Shay nodded. "I'd feel a lot better if you weren't living in tunnels. Look, you've seen the kind of money tomb raiding brings in. Even if we didn't get the big score in Montana, you still got a nice cut of the money the Professor paid me. You're not some poor urchin who needs to steal to survive anymore. I get that it can take money to get established, but you have that now, more than enough, and Montana's not going to be the last job."

Alison smiled at Lily. "Before I went to the School of Necessary Magic, I didn't think about magic other than my sight. Now I can do all sorts of spells. Maybe if you get established, you know, above ground, you all could look into enrolling at the school."

Lily nodded slowly. "I'll have to mention it to Harry."

"Pizza is beyond cooking," Peyton began. He was strutting around in an apron and a tall chef's hat. "Pizza is a combination of conventional cooking and baking, which really means that it's chemistry. A master pizza chef is a master chemist. No, an alchemist!"

Shay chuckled. James just watched, his attention riveted. He might be more of a barbeque man, but cooking was one of the few things besides ass-kicking he actually cared about.

Peyton knelt by the oven. "Timing is everything. The proper amount of heat for the proper amount of time. That subtle transfer of energy and how it transforms all the individual ingredients." He took a deep breath. "Even the smallest timing mistake, a little too early or a little too late, throws it all off."

James' stomach rumbled. "Not telling you to rush your shit, but are we ever gonna eat?"

Lily and Alison nodded their agreement.

"You don't rush a masterpiece," Peyton intoned, holding up his hand. "It's almost ready. Just give me a moment. Almost there. Almost there." He grinned. "It's ready."

He grabbed his pizza paddle and opened the oven,

stuck the paddle under the pizza, and carefully lifted it out of the oven. "Behold, the ultimate in pepperoni pizza, using only the finest ingredients. No magic has been used, ladies and gentlemen, only pure skill to bring you this treasure."

Shay smiled. She'd noticed a slight change in Peyton in the last couple of weeks. She'd worried that he'd spent too much time mourning his scumbag brother, but after the surprise of the first few days, the goofy man seemed more relaxed. He might not be ready or even all that interested in reestablishing contact with the rest of his family, but, much like Shay, he finally seemed ready to move on with the rest of his life.

I know what it's like to have a death threat constantly hanging over your head. You can't really live if you think you're gonna die any day.

James pulled away from her to inspect the pizza, scratching his chin.

"Maybe we can get you doing pizza and not just barbeque," Shay suggested.

The bounty hunter grunted and shook his head. "I haven't even mastered barbeque yet. Adding something else would just be annoying."

Peyton grinned. "Then I shall remain the Pizza King forever."

Alison smirked. "Your Highness, we peasants are starving."

"Of course, of course. As a royal, I understand all too well the concept of noblesse oblige. One moment." He turned.

A fast-moving mass of orange fur charged toward him, yowling. Osiris ran through his legs, and Peyton stumbled.

The pizza was jolted into the air. The hacker recovered his footing and spun with the paddle, catching the pizza an inch or two before it hit the ground.

He let out a sigh of relief. "That was too damned close."

Lily shrugged. "I say we order in. Didn't you tell me there's some sort of evil delivery company?"

James frowned. "What evil delivery company?"

Shay laughed. "They're not evil. They're just discrete."

Peyton slowly stood, his gaze locked on the pizza. "The Pizza King doesn't summon aid from foreign lands. Besides, I still have it, and another one will be ready in just a few minutes."

"Let's just eat," Shay suggested. She smiled as she looked from James to Peyton, Lily, and Alison.

I have a man I love. I have a friend and two girls I care about. Daughters? Maybe. And for the first time in my life, I want to live for someone other than me.

About an hour later, James nodded toward his F-350 in the loading bay. "I need to show Shay something."

Peyton eyed him. "In the middle of the night?"

"Yeah." James shrugged. "I'll swing by later to pick up Alison, or you can drop her back at my place if she wants to go home earlier than that."

Shay looked at her boyfriend and Peyton, confused about what James had planned. "What about Lily?"

The girl smiled. "I was planning on crashing here tonight anyway."

James tugged on her arm. "Let's go. I've done some complicated shit, and I don't want it to be a total waste."

Shay let him lead her to his truck, still confused. James Brownstone was many things, but he didn't tend to be mysterious. Mysterious wasn't simple, and simplicity was his second religion after Catholicism.

Complicated shit, huh?

"Do I need any extra gear?" she asked.

James grunted. "Nah, nothing like that. Just come with me. You'll like it. Maybe. I don't know. The podcast said you'll like it."

"The podcast?"

Shay shot a shrug at Peyton, Lily, and Alison before getting into the truck.

James hopped inside and started the F350. "Just figured it'd be good to spend some time away from the kids. You'll see. You should like it."

"Not gonna tell me what's up?"

He shook his head. "Trying to give you an 'experience.'"

Shay laughed. "Oh, this better not end with me having to strangle a man."

"It shouldn't." James frowned. "I hope." He rubbed his neck.

***

Shay tapped her foot impatiently as the elevator kept rising. With her most recent experience in high-rise buildings and elevators ending in her shooting several people, she couldn't help it when her heart sped up.

James obviously wouldn't lead her to a dangerous situation without telling her to be prepared, but she just couldn't figure out why he'd take her to the top of a very tall building.

She winced at a sudden thought.

Please don't tell me that James suddenly wants to take up parkour. That would be...interesting, but this is definitely not the place for a rookie to start.

The bounty hunter's face remained blank, and he kept his words to a minimum. Whatever he had planned, he was going for maximum surprise.

The elevator dinged, and James stepped out and pointed to the stairwell access. "Got to hit the roof through the stairs."

Shay's hands twitched, but it wasn't as if she were completely unarmed. She did have her loaded 9mm and one of her adamantine knives. If she were dealing with only a small number of enemies, it wouldn't be a problem.

Her gaze flicked to James' chest. She wondered if he were bonded to his amulet already.

Okay, okay. Calm down. James isn't taking me to a surprise battle. That's not his style.

Shay chuckled a little. When she thought about it, a surprise battle actually sounded fun.

They made it to the top of the stairs. James stepped to the door and Shay instinctively tensed, remembering the gunshots at the ARCO Tower.

The bounty hunter pulled open the door, and no bullets flew. Instead, she could hear light classical music playing.

"Huh?"

James held the door for her and motioned her toward the roof. Shay passed through the door.

No gangsters. No witches. No frogmen.

There was a blanket surrounded by candles. Chocolate-covered strawberries were piled high on a silver tray in the center, along with two glasses and an open bottle of champagne. A small speaker on the edge of the blanket provided the music.

James grunted. "I got a little worried when the news said it might be cloudy tonight. It would have ruined the view."

Shay walked toward the blanket and smiled. Judging by the elevator, they were over seventy stories up. The vastness of Los Angeles lay around them—the tall buildings and the lights. The view from ARCO Tower had been impressive, but this was like being a Greek goddess on Olympus who could look down on the works of the mortals.

"The podcast said that women like nice views and surprise desserts." James shrugged.

Shay smiled as she turned 360 degrees, taking in the view from every angle. "It's definitely romantic." She laughed. "I guess you *do* learn things from listening to those podcasts."

She knelt on the blanket and popped a chocolate-covered strawberry into her mouth. She let the flavor linger on her tongue before she started chewing.

James knelt beside her. "I wanted to do something nice. We're both so busy, always kicking ass. This shit means a lot more to me than just sex."

Shay snickered. Only James Brownstone could get away with referring to their relationship as "this shit" and have it come out sounding romantic.

"I know that, dumbass. I also know you're still getting used to it." She shrugged. "Shit, *I'm* still getting used to it. You kept yourself away from other people because you thought you were weird, but I was a ruthless killer for half my life. I prided myself on not giving a shit about anyone and never relying on anyone."

James looked at her. "And now?"

"And now I love you. I care about Alison, Lily, and Peyton, too. Fuck, even my friends who made my place smell for weeks. I care about them." Shay sucked in a breath.

I say I care about him, but I keep shit from him, shit he deserves to know. I keep telling myself it's for his own good, but how can he keep himself safe if he doesn't even know about the threat?

James frowned. "Something wrong?"

"There's something I need to tell you."

His eyes widened, and panic covered his face. "Oh shit."

She punched him in the arm. "I'm not pregnant, dumbass, if that's what you're worried about."

Visible relief followed. "Still getting used to my first daughter, is all."

Shay rolled her eyes. "It's nothing like that."

"What then?"

She took a few deep breaths. "Before I confirmed everything about your alien identity, I'd started looking into some other alien stuff."

"What alien stuff?"

"I found a stone on a job in Mexico. This possessed elf had it. I thought he was possessed by a demon, but I don't know. Since then, I've had several more jobs or encounters involving these stones. They aren't magic, from what I can tell, but they have writing on them. Writing that I established doesn't come from our planet or Oriceran."

James nodded slowly but kept silent.

"I've been able to link these stones to your amulet. So wherever your homeworld is, your people have probably visited before. Not only that, they might still be here among us."

He furrowed his brow. "How do you know?"

"Partial translations of some of the writing on the stones suggests they're here, or at least they have been recently."

James frowned. "Why didn't you tell me any of this?"

"Because I also found out that I'm not the only one interested in it. The Professor and Correk are, which isn't such a big deal, but they aren't the only ones either."

"Who else?"

Shay looked away. "The government. The federal government. There are secret projects, Ragnarok and Nephilim. The government knows non-Oriceran aliens are here, and they're worried about them. They have this asshole, Durand, working on collecting alien artifacts. I've tangled with him a few times. That raid I just went to in Montana for the Professor? There was an alien artifact there, too. Another stone. Some CIA guy named Daniel Goldstein is interested in this stuff, too, but I don't think he's working for the other faction."

"Shit," James rumbled. "So everyone knew about this but me?"

Shay put her hand on his shoulder. "I was worried that

if I told you, you might go knocking some heads. You're tough, but you can't take on the entire government."

The bounty hunter chuckled. "Why does everyone always think I'm going break everything and throw people through windows?"

"It's not exactly like you're a man famous for measured and calm responses to people who piss you off."

"The government fucked with me over Alison, but from what we found out, it doesn't sound like that had anything to do with this shit." He frowned deeper. "Or did it?"

Shay shook her head. "Nope, but I'm worried that if these Ragnarok or Nephilim assholes ever figure out you're an alien, they might lock you up or try to drag you off to a lab somewhere."

James smirked. "Love to see them try." He shrugged. "Look, not gonna announce my background to the world, but if they haven't figured it out by now, they probably won't."

The tomb raider blew out a long breath. "Now you know the truth. You pissed? I kept Lily from you, and now this. I wouldn't blame you if you were mad."

He shrugged. "Nah. Not like you told me the government had a secret barbeque project and you'd been keeping it from me."

Shay laughed. "You *would* be more pissed at that, wouldn't you?"

"Just saying."

She blinked a few times. "Now that you know that your people might be around, are you gonna go look for them? Your people? Your family?"

"Why the fuck would I bother?" James patted his chest.

"Whispy Doom is useful, but he's kind of a bloodthirsty asshole. I don't know if my people are the kind of folks I even want to know. And as for family, some aliens I've never met aren't my family. Fuck that. It's people like you, Alison, Father McCartney, Trey, and Mack." He shook his head. "I don't give a shit about the past anymore. I only care about the future."

Shay smiled warmly. "Lately I keep thinking back to when I saved Peyton. You know why I did it?"

James shrugged. "Because you needed help?"

"Yeah, basically. That was it. He was nothing to me, just a tool that I threatened into working for me. When I met you, I was impressed by your skills, but I didn't want to go on jobs with you. I didn't want to have to rely on anyone I couldn't control, and if there's one thing it's a bad idea to do, it's controlling James Brownstone." Shay sighed. "But things changed. I started giving a shit about Peyton, and not just as a risk to me. I started wanting to spend more time with you. I felt bad for Alison and wanted her to have a better future."

James listened, a smile playing on his lips.

Shay stood and started pacing. "The UCLA thing was just supposed to be a cover—an excuse—but I liked it. Started caring there, too. When I gave my first lecture, it felt almost as good as when I had a solid kill. I realized there was something there, a way to have satisfaction with life that didn't just involve me proving I'm the toughest bitch on the planet." She pointed to the sky. "It's beautiful, even washed-out as it is because of the light pollution in Los Angeles. That's what I forgot. How to live or see any beauty in life."

She continued staring into the sky for a moment, taking it all in. All those years, all those lives, both saved and killed. All of it had woven together in a tight tapestry to form the woman called Shay Carson who now lived in Los Angeles, and that woman finally could imagine what it would be like to grow old with someone she loved.

Is this what life is? Planning for the future, not just making plans to survive? I thought I had a life plan before, but what I really had was a survival plan.

"You're young," James rumbled. "You turned your life around. No big deal."

She stopped pacing and laughed down at James. "That's just it. I never planned to. I never wanted to turn my life around. Now I find myself wondering what my friends are up to, what the next parkour course I'm gonna run with Free-to-Move is. What the hell happened? I used to be alone, and I liked it that way."

James shook his head. "No, you didn't."

"Huh? I'm pretty sure—"

He quieted her with a raised hand. "You *thought* you liked it that way, just like I thought I liked being alone. Nothing but the job, barbeque, and Leeroy. Alison showed me there was more to life, and then you showed me even more. I'd been locked in a closet my entire life, but I'd convinced myself it was a mansion I chose to live in. You did the same thing."

Shay blinked and again knelt beside James. "You say something smart every now and again."

James grunted. "I try."

She offered him a soft smile. "You really know how to get to a girl."

"Well, *one* girl. If you dump me, I think I'm giving up on understanding women."

"Where do we go from here?"

James shrugged. "I'm James Brownstone, Scourge of Harriken. You're Shay Carson, tomb raider. We do whatever the hell we want, and we go anywhere we want. I just want to do it together."

Shay filled both the glasses with champagne and handed him a glass.

She raised her glass. "It's not a bad life."

James raised his. "Nope. Not a bad life at all."

"I love you, you know."

"Good, I love you, too. Does that mean you'll stop calling me dumbass if I do something you don't like?"

Shay grinned. "A girl's got to have a little fun."

With this story, Shay Carson wraps up her own series but will be around kicking ass with Brownstone somewhere in the Oriceran sphere. She's a fun character because she's equal parts dangerous and protective of those she loves – and that circle has continuously expanded, much to her surprise. New series are starting up – we don't rest here for very long. Five minutes here, a minute or two there. The Daniel Codex will be coming your way soon (remember him?)

Meanwhile, I've moved into the big new dream house and in the past week it's been a steady stream of tradesmen coming in to repair something. Yesterday my old laptop that has served me valiantly joined in and started to let me know it was going any minute. I took the hint and went out to Best Buy. I asked the young millennial what computer he would get, and he said, "I build my own." That aside, he also gave good advice.

Today, the hose behind the washing machine sprung a leak and flooded the laundry room. The movers who put the hole there came running and helped clean it up and the builder came running to help diagnose the problem. I found out I can still move with lightning speed and finally unpacked all the towels. It was a good reminder that things may turn upside down but there are good people around who run to help.

Tomorrow is my birthday – my last year in my 50's. I like to think of myself as a senior babe. I'm going to be whooping it up with my three 'brothers' – Michael, Craig and Steve – in Las Vegas because that's how we roll. Def Leppard and Journey! Frankly, my 50's have been the best years yet and things just keep getting better. I like to think of myself as a strong finisher.

I'm looking forward to settling into the new house and figuring out where I left the remote… I'm doing my best not to suspect the good dog, Lois. It'll turn up one of these days.

Until then, hope everyone is having a good year as well. For my birthday I wish for you peace and joy and a year that unfolds with all good things. More adventures to follow.

THANK YOU for not only reading this story, but these *Author Notes* as well!

Shay's story isn't finished, but it's over for now. I have to admit we had a bit of trouble trying to figure out how to interweave Shay's and Brownstone's stories, and even now, we are working to fix (or maybe by the time you read this, we will have already fixed) parts of the first three books.

While Shay enjoyed a HUGE amount of support, there were a few comments about how much the characters (Brownstone and Shay and to some degree Alison) hide from each other. I'd like to answer a bit of the why.

When I created these three characters, they were all independent. Shay is a (sort of) recovering killer, Alison has lost her mom and her dad is actively trying to sell her, while Brownstone is a bounty hunter with a life focus of keeping everything as simple as he can.

Well, sharing isn't simple, trusting when your friends might kill you doesn't provide much opportunity to extend trust, and when your dad is evil, it's hard to allow your heart to be vulnerable.

So, my opinion is that they might refrain from telling each other for personal reasons. Not wanting to hurt someone (best of intentions, poor execution), privacy concerns, not wanting to be hurt again. It takes time to heal from wounds.

Between the books about Brownstone and Shay, we have six Shays and nine Brownstones in the same timeline as about 2.1 School of Necessary Magic stories. As Alison's stories move forward, Brownstone's won't catch up. Shay is being pulled into Brownstone full time for now, because the interweaving of the stories is hurting our poor little author heads.

Believe it or not, this shit is *hard,* and we want a bit of a vacation from the truly magnificently hard stuff. (Ok, I can't rope Martha into this excuse without asking her, so for *me* this shit was hard and hurting my head... And everyone helping us write these books was hurting as well.

Even Lynne, editor magus was threatening to quit if we kept it up. Hell, I just realized I could have blamed all of this on her. (Editor's note: Just try it, big guy! I'll write you into a few scenes of Kurtherian Endgame with pink hair bows and frilly knickers—drinking *Pepsi.*)

<MIKE EDIT AFTER EDITOR EDIT: No one would believe that version of me ;-) >

Dammit.

Oh well, never waste any words, so I guess the truth is going to stay in the *Author Notes.*

Ummm, I'd blame Zen Master Walking ™ (Stephen Campbell) but he is the one who takes all of our work and pulls it into Vellum for final production, so he can edit my *Author Notes* and I'd find out what he said no faster than you—and it might not be kind, so no blaming him without cause.

If you love Shay, (or any book by any author) feel free to plug it with a good review. It helps us sell more of these books, and fund my Coke (Coca-Cola) habit!

Ad Aeternitatem,

Michael Anderle

Waking Magic (1) - Release of Magic (2) - Protection of Magic (3) - Rule of Magic (4) - Dealing in Magic (5) - Theft of Magic (6) - Enemies of Magic (7) - Guardians of Magic (8)

The Soul Stone Mage Series

* Sarah Noffke and Martha Carr *

House of Enchanted (1) - The Dark Forest (2) - Mountain of Truth (3) - Land of Terran (4) - New Egypt (5) - Lancothy (6) - Virgo (7)

The Kacy Chronicles

* A.L. Knorr and Martha Carr *

Descendant (1) - Ascendant (2) - Combatant (3) - Transcendent (4)

The Midwest Magic Chronicles

* Flint Maxwell and Martha Carr*

The Midwest Witch (1) - The Midwest Wanderer (2) - The Midwest Whisperer (3) - The Midwest War (4)

The Fairhaven Chronicles

* with S.M. Boyce *

Glow (1) - Shimmer (2) - Ember (3) - Nightfall (4)